Mail-Order Wings

Mail-Order Wings

by BEATRICE GORMLEY

illustrated by Emily Arnold McCully

E. P. DUTTON • NEW YORK

Library of Congress Cataloging in Publication Data

Gormley, Beatrice.   Mail-order wings.

Summary: Nine-year-old Andrea orders wings through the
mail with a guarantee to fly. Incredibly, they work,
but there is a frightening side effect.
[1. Flight—Fiction]   I. McCully, Emily Arnold.   II. Title.
PZ7.G6696Mai   1981   [Fic]   81-3283
ISBN 0-525-34450-0   AACR2

Published in the United States by E. P. Dutton Inc.,
2 Park Avenue, New York, N.Y. 10016

Editor: Ann Durell   Designer: Claire Counihan

Printed in the U.S.A.

10 9 8 7 6 5 4 3

to Katie and Jenny

Contents

🪶1🪶

I Want To Fly

Andrea knelt on the floor of her bedroom, reorganizing her comic books.

She loved her room, the only bedroom on the third floor of the house. It was built out of part of the attic, with an east-facing dormer window. This room had two great advantages.

First, it was up so high that Andrea could see far out over the town—over trees and neighbors' roofs to her friend Lauren's house, or to the school six blocks away. On sunny days like today, she could even glimpse the shining pond in the bird sanctuary. The second advantage was peace and quiet. Andrea needed peace and quiet for projects like making her own paper dolls, or studying her bird nest collection, or reorganizing her comic books.

Until today she had kept the comics in series: a pile

1

of *Bugs Bunny,* a pile of *Dennis the Menace,* a pile of *Little Lulu,* and so on. But this afternoon she had a better idea: she would sort them according to how well she liked them. Then she would have only three big piles, which would fit better in her bookcase.

Three piles seemed right. A Favorite pile, a Pretty Good pile, and an Okay pile. She didn't have any comic books that she thought of as Not Very Good or Terrible.

That wasn't exactly true. Andrea picked up the end of one dark brown ponytail and sucked it nervously. She did have one Terrible comic book. She had just thrown it into her wastebasket. Now, for some reason, she wasn't sure she wanted to throw it away.

That was silly. Andrea went to her desk and wrote out three labels: *Favorite, Pretty Good,* and *Okay.* She set the three piles of comic books on a shelf of the bookcase and taped the labels onto the edge of the shelf.

As she pressed down the last label, the bookcase wobbled and one of the paper dolls on top pitched headfirst into the robin's nest. Andrea sighed and set the girl doll back on its feet. She was pleased with these paper dolls, which she had drawn and cut out of cardboard and made clothes for herself, but it was very hard to get them to stand up right. The extra piece of cardboard propping them from behind didn't quite do the trick.

The robin's nest seemed to be coming apart, too. Andrea replaced a stick that had fallen out, setting it in with a glob of paste for good measure.

The paper dolls were a family like hers, a mother

2

and a father and a daughter. Except that her own family also had her big brother, Jim. "Why doesn't the girl have a big brother?" Lauren had asked last weekend. "Or a little brother, like mine?"

Andrea had shrugged. "She doesn't really need a brother."

The story in the Terrible comic book was about a family. She couldn't help thinking about it. Unwillingly, Andrea pulled the comic out of the used tissues and pencil shavings in her wastebasket and looked at it again.

Chilling Tales, it said on the cover. The letters were green and purple and sort of dripping. The worst story, "No Longer Human," was about a boy who changed into a huge beetle.

It wasn't his fault—he just woke up one morning and discovered he was now a beetle. He tried to ask his father and mother and sister for help, but he could only make beetle noises. And they hated him. They didn't want to believe that this disgusting insect was really their son and brother.

They locked him in his bedroom and kept him there. He got more and more frantic, until finally he tried to break out one morning when they brought him food. That frightened his father so much that he threw a lamp at the beetle, breaking his shell.

After that the boy-beetle stayed quietly in his room. The wound in his shell became badly infected, and he grew sicker and sicker until he died. Then his mother told the trash collector to haul his body to the dump.

If only she hadn't bought this comic book and read

this story. How horrible not to be yourself! How unthinkably horrible to see your own family turn away from you in fear and disgust! Andrea tried not to think about it, but the story seemed to crouch in the back of her mind, waiting to be remembered.

Every time she thought of it she wanted to shout, "No! It didn't happen!" Of course it *hadn't* happened, but somehow it seemed as real to Andrea as anything that had.

Maybe she wouldn't throw that comic away yet, but she wasn't going to keep it on her bookshelf, either. She was about to hurl it onto the top shelf of her closet when she noticed a picture on the back cover.

This picture wasn't horrible at all. It showed a girl with red and blue and yellow wings swooping over the treetops, laughing. On a nearby branch a robin was watching her with its beak open, almost falling off its perch in amazement.

The picture was part of an advertisement. "Fly with your own wings!" it said. "Send for easy-to-assemble Wonda-Wings kit." At the bottom of the page there was a form to fill out and send "with check or money order to:

> Aero-Joy Products, Inc.
> New Heights, N.J. 07189

Do not send cash thru mail."

Andrea studied the picture for a moment. Then she stepped over a half-finished jigsaw puzzle on her floor to look out the window.

For just an instant she imagined herself floating on

the warm September wind, high above the front lawn and the lilac hedge, over Maple Avenue, over the television aerial on the house across the street. It was a wonderful, free, powerful feeling. Then she laughed quickly, as if someone had caught her having such a childish thought. She knew people couldn't fly. Any four-year-old knew that. Still . . . no one needed to find out that she sent away for the wings. She had her own money.

How much was the kit? "A stupendous value at only $5.98!" She had a lot more money than that. Her grandmother in Florida had sent her ten dollars for her birthday and she hadn't had a chance to spend it yet.

Of course Andrea knew that advertisements didn't always tell the exact truth about things. She had been gypped before. The worst disappointment had been the time she sent in her $1.89 for a Treasure Chest of Magic. "Astound your friends!" the advertisement had said. "Dozens of mystifying illusions!" The picture had shown a golden jewel-encrusted chest with cards and rabbits and Aladdin's lamps spilling out of it.

But when the package came and Andrea tore it open, the treasure chest inside was very small and made of cheap plastic, and all the props for magic tricks looked about as convincing as the prizes in cereal packages. Andrea didn't bother trying to astound her friends with that junk. She didn't like being laughed at. Feeling sorry for her, Dad had taught her how to pull a quarter out of someone's ear. That partly made up for being cheated, but not completely.

Andrea examined the Wonda-Wings advertisement more closely. "Absolute money-back guarantee if not completely satisfied," it said. What could she lose?

Andrea took the comic book to her desk and began to fill out the form:

Yes! I want to fly!

Please rush __1__ Wonda–Wings kits to

Andrea Reve	10	9
(name)	(size)	(age)

19 Maple Avenue
_____
(street)

Rushfield ,	Mass .	01443
(city)	(state)	(zip)

My check _____ money order _____ for $5.98 is enclosed.

Here Andrea stopped. She didn't have a checkbook, but Mother did. Andrea could give Mother the money, and Mother could write the check. That's what they'd done when she sent away for the Treasure Chest of Magic.

Except that Mother wouldn't do it this time—Andrea was pretty sure she wouldn't. "I can't let you waste your money like that, Andy," she would say. "Didn't you learn anything from the Treasure Chest episode?" Dad would be even harder to persuade than Mother.

That left Jim, who was sixteen. Andrea didn't think he had a checking account, but he would probably know how to get a money order. Would he make fun of her? He might. When he noticed her at all he treated her as if she were a silly puppy or something. On the other hand, she didn't think he would care whether she wasted her money or not. It was worth a try.

Andrea cut the form out of the comic book, pushed back her chair, and tossed *Chilling Tales* onto the top shelf of her closet. Then she hurried to the window. Pushing up the screen, she leaned out the window so she could see the driveway. There was Jim, shooting baskets.

Andrea pattered down the two flights of stairs and ran out the kitchen door to the driveway. Jim was hooking a shot at the basket. "Hey, Jim," she yelled, and he missed.

Frowning, he caught the ball as it slid off the garage. "What d'you want, shrimp?"

"Well, I was just wondering if you would help me get a money order."

Jim didn't answer—he just stood there, one hand in his pocket and the other bouncing the basketball at his side.

"I need it to send away for something."

Jim shrugged. "Give the money to Mother. She'll write a check for you." He turned away, rose on the balls of his feet, and shoved the basketball into the air in one neat motion so that it dropped cleanly through the basket. "Nice, Reve, nice."

"No, she won't." Andrea stepped in front of him to

8

make him pay attention. "She'd say it was a waste of money."

"Oh, good. So you want me to drive you to the post office to get the money order so Mother can get ticked at *me* for helping you waste your money." He looked at her with one eyebrow raised. "What're you sending away for, anyway? A nuclear weapon kit? Let's see." He reached out for the form in her hand.

Andrea stepped back, holding the form behind her. "Why can't you just—" She stopped. "The post office? That's where you get money orders?"

"Yeah, didn't you know that?" Jim looked at her sharply, then twirled the basketball up into the air and caught it, smiling to himself. "Well, Mother, I just blew it. Sorry. Sport, you're smarter than I thought." He dribbled the basketball down the driveway.

Andrea ran back into the house and all the way up to her room, skipping every other stair. Hooray! She could send for the wings by herself. She took the cork from her pig bank and coaxed out the ten-dollar bill with a pencil, stuffed the money into her shorts pocket, and dashed back downstairs. Grabbing an envelope and stamp from Mother's desk, she ran out to the garage to get her bike. As she wheeled it down the driveway Jim called, "Way to go, squirt! Waste that money!"

Mission accomplished. Andrea was pumping back up the rise on Maple Avenue, almost home, when she saw her mother's yellow Rabbit turning in the driveway. She was coming home from teaching her class at the junior college. Getting out of the car with an armful of books and folders, Mother caught sight of Andrea and waved. Andrea waved back, pedaling past the hedge and into the driveway.

"Warm, isn't it?" The mild wind lifted Mother's dark bangs from her forehead. "How was your day, Andy?" She waited while Andrea parked her bike in the garage.

"Oh, fine. How about you?" Andrea felt a little guilty, even though she wasn't telling a lie.

"Fine. We had a terrific discussion in class today." Mother smiled, but she seemed to be thinking about something else. She put an arm around Andrea's shoulder as they walked into the kitchen. "Hi, Jim. Warm, isn't it?"

Jim was standing at the sink, drinking water. "Yeah. Hi. Can I use the car?"

Mother put her books and folders down on the kitchen table. "You can probably have the car this afternoon. But first I want to tell you both something, while we're here together." She glanced at Andrea to include her. "I just wanted to let you know that Dad and I will be going to Nantucket for a few days next month."

Jim, leaning against the sink, looked at Mother sharply. Andrea studied her face, too. There was a note of uneasiness in Mother's voice, and her usually direct blue eyes were looking at the refrigerator.

"Am I going to stay with Lauren?" That was the usual arrangement when Andrea's parents went away for a weekend.

"Am I supposed to stay with Skip?" There was suspicion in Jim's voice.

"Well, no, I didn't think I should ask your friends' parents to keep you for so long. We'll be gone longer than usual this time—from Thursday morning to Tuesday night, to be exact. I thought it would be better if you stayed here."

"Oh, that's okay." Jim's face brightened. "We'll be fine."

"Six whole days?" exclaimed Andrea. She slumped into a chair. She couldn't believe Mother would leave her with Jim for six days.

"I'm sure you will be fine," said Mother to Jim, "because Aunt Bets has offered to stay with you while we're gone."

"Aunt Bets? We don't have an Aunt Bets." Jim folded his arms and scowled. "Anyway, I don't need anyone to stay with me."

"I don't want to stay with Jim and I don't want to stay with Aunt Bets," said Andrea loudly. Either way it sounded like a pretty dismal week.

"You don't even know Aunt Bets." Mother had started the discussion in a reasonable tone of voice, but now she sounded irritated. "She isn't actually your aunt. She's Dad's aunt, so she's your great-aunt. We don't see her often because she lives near New York. But I've been feeling bad because her husband died a couple of years ago—I don't know if you remember when Dad and I went down for the funeral—and she's really pretty much by herself except for friends."

Mother glanced up, met Jim's stony stare, and went

on hastily. "Well, anyway, I called her this morning to see how she was and if she wanted to come up here for a visit sometime, and it came out in the conversation that Phil and I were planning this vacation on Nantucket, and she said she'd really like to come and stay with you while we are gone."

Andrea had a vision of a little old lady with a bun and laced black shoes sitting at their kitchen table and smiling sadly. For six whole days. She looked at Jim.

"That's a super idea," he said to Mother sarcastically. "Only why don't you take Aunt Bets to Nantucket with you?" He put his hands behind his head and looked down at her from half-closed lids.

Mother waved a hand helplessly. "Actually I tried to talk her into visiting while we were here, but she wouldn't hear of it. I think it makes her feel good to think she's doing something for us. And she especially wanted to spend time getting to know both of you."

"Well, I especially don't want to spend any time getting to know her," growled Jim. "Why don't you call her back and tell her that?"

"Aunt Bets isn't that bad. In fact, she's rather interesting." Mother was back to her reasonable voice. "It won't hurt you to be exposed to her for a few days."

"That and chicken pox." Jim looked really angry now. His chin stuck out and his voice rose. "Why do I have to stay with Aunt Bets so *you* can feel good about being nice to her? The whole idea *stinks*!"

Andrea stared at Jim's red face, forgetting to be upset herself. In a distasteful kind of way it was fascinat-

ing to watch someone that big throwing a temper fit. Like Lauren's two-year-old brother. She almost expected Jim to yell "Me want!" and drum his heels on the floor.

"That's enough." Mother's own cheeks were pink. "Aunt Bets is staying with you and Andrea while we're gone. It's all settled. And I expect you to be civil to her. And that's the end of the discussion."

Jim's heel slammed into the cupboard door under the sink. "Yes, ma'am; yes, ma'am." He banged his glass down on the counter. "I'm so glad I live in a free country, ma'am. May I have permission to leave the room, ma'am? Oh, thank you, ma'am." He stalked out of the kitchen.

"Oh, for pity's sake," said Mother. She sat down and put her feet up on another chair.

Andrea gazed thoughtfully after Jim. She didn't want to stay with Aunt Bets, either, but why throw a fit about it? "What's the matter with Jim?"

Mother looked at Andrea in surprise. Then she smiled and let out a long sigh. "Hormones. Jim has a lot of hormones coursing around in his bloodstream, making him grow and so on. They give him feelings that are hard to control. It happens to everybody about that age."

"You mean Jim can't help acting like that?" asked Andrea unbelievingly.

Mother snorted. "Oh, he can help it, all right. He has free will." Her blue eyes sparkled fiercely. "Human beings always have a choice." Then she smiled ruefully at Andrea. "Even when they're dealing with Aunt

Bets." She held out her arms. "Come here a minute, Andy."

Andrea got up and walked slowly over to her mother. She was angry herself, she remembered, that Mother and Dad were going away for six whole days, leaving her with Jim and some gloomy old lady. But it was nice to stand leaning against her mother, her cheek brushing Mother's soft dark hair. Andrea breathed in the faint scent of her hand lotion.

2

Wonda-Wings

"Andy is a doo-doo bird, Andy is a doo-doo bird." Julie Dodd was chanting as she skipped behind Andrea on the sidewalk. Lauren wasn't actually chanting, but she was skipping with Julie and laughing.

Andrea clutched the carton containing her bird nest collection and walked a little faster. It was all Miss Silvano's fault. "I'm sure the class would love to see your bird nest collection, Andrea," she had said. "Please bring it to school." Why had Andrea trusted her? Miss Silvano didn't know a thing about what kids liked.

Andrea had wanted to believe the other kids would like her bird nests. They *would* have liked them, if they weren't such stupid idiots.

At first the kids had been interested, crowding around the science table and reaching out to feel the nests. Each one was different: a messy sticks-and-leaves robin's nest, a small, deep red-eyed vireo's nest, and a baglike oriole's nest.

Then Scott, the loudmouth of the class, had jerked his hand away. "Oh, no! I touched bird doo-doo!"

Everyone pulled back and stared at the white splotch on the robin's nest. "It's just paste," said Andrea. "Birds keep their nests clean." But no one paid any attention.

Julie Dodd snickered. "Andrea plays with bird doo-doo." Several other children laughed, including Lauren. Andrea had never liked Julie.

"Everyone in your seats," said Miss Silvano sharply. "If you're going to act like kindergartners, I can't give you any more time to look at Andrea's fine collection."

At recess it had been worse. Scott had run past her down the slope, shouting so the other boys would hear, "Hey, Andy! Let's see your fine doo-doo collection!"

Andrea didn't care so much about the boys, who never played with girls anyway. But when the girls started a game of tag, Julie kept saying things like "What's that white spot on your pants, Andy?" and "Don't touch me! Yuck! You've got it on your hands!" Pretty soon all the girls were screaming and running away from her. Even Lauren.

Andrea did not look back, but she knew Julie and Lauren were still behind her on the sidewalk. Julie began to talk in a smooth, phony interviewer's voice. "Tell me, Miss Reve, just how did you get this *fine* collection?" Then Julie answered herself in another voice, a high, breathy voice that was supposed to be Andrea's: "Well, I just—first I collected some robin doo-doo

17

. . . and then I collected some oriole doo-doo. . . ." There were choking and scuffling sounds. They were falling over each other laughing.

Julie didn't live in Andrea and Lauren's neighborhood. She must be going home for the afternoon with Lauren. Andrea hoped they would have a wonderful time together. Maybe they would choke and die laughing in each other's arms.

Honk.

Andrea heard the bicycle-horn sound in the sky. She did not look up, but she knew it was a flock of Canada geese.

HONK honk honk honk HONK. A whole orchestra of bicycle horns tuning up. If Andrea and Lauren had been walking home together, they would have tried to count the geese before the V-shaped flock flew out of sight.

"And what are your plans for the future, Miss Reve?" Julie was still having a wonderful time with her interview imitation. "Well, in the future I hope to collect some goose"—Julie's voice sputtered with laughter—"some goose doo-doo."

Andrea clenched her teeth and imagined herself rising up in the air on loudly beating wings. Above Julie, above her so-called friend Lauren, so high that their stupid giggles dwindled away to mouse squeaks in the silence of the sky.

Andrea heard Lauren gasping with laughter. She couldn't stand it any longer. She whirled around and charged at the other girls as if she were going to bash into them with the carton. "Shut up!"

They stopped, looking startled.

Then Andrea knew she was going to start crying, and she turned and ran up the sidewalk as fast as she could—awkwardly because she had to hold the bird nest carton with both hands. Tears dripped saltily into her mouth. She ran down Winter Street and straight through the intersection at Cross Street, hardly looking to see whether any cars were coming. She ran another block, gasping, to Maple Avenue, crossed the street and turned left.

She was almost home—she had to pull herself together. Andrea glanced back toward Winter Street. Julie and Lauren were nowhere in sight. She put down the carton, found an old tissue in her jeans pocket, and wiped her face. If Mother had been home Andrea could have come in crying, but she couldn't let Jim or Aunt Bets see her like this. She picked up the box again and marched up the rise to her driveway.

The big maple tree at the end of the driveway was turning color. Half of it was still green, but the other half was a brilliant red. Andrea stopped to stare at it, forgetting for a moment what an awful day it had been. Then her eyes moved from the tree to the strange car in the driveway, and her heart sank again. Aunt Bets was in there.

In fact, Andrea saw someone waving excitedly to her from the bay window in the kitchen. But was that Aunt Bets? That tall woman with reddish blonde hair?

Just as Andrea came up to the kitchen door, it opened and the woman burst forth, holding out her arms. "Well, Andrea, dear!"

19

Andrea stared in amazement at the purplish eye shadow and forceful chin, the lilac-colored dress and high-heeled sandals. "Hi . . . Aunt Bets?"

Aunt Bets seized Andrea by the shoulders, surrounding her with a cloud of cologne, and leaned over the bird nest carton to kiss her on both cheeks. Then she held her off at arm's length. "Philip's little girl! But don't you look like your mama, with those blue eyes and dark hair." She peered into the carton. "And is this a special project from school?" Aunt Bets put her hand on Andrea's back and steered her into the kitchen. "Such pink cheeks, hasn't she, James? She'll never need to wear rouge."

Jim was standing at the kitchen counter in front of the toaster. He did not answer or turn around. He must still be mad about Aunt Bets staying with them.

Andrea noticed a large package wrapped in brown paper on the kitchen table. She wondered if it was something Aunt Bets had brought, but her great-aunt sat down without saying anything about it. "Well!" Aunt Bets smiled at Andrea enthusiastically. "This is a good chance for us to get acquainted. I said to your mother, 'Elise,' I said, 'I would be *delighted* to take a little time off from work to stay with the children.' "

Andrea put her carton down on the table and glanced at Jim's back, hunched over the counter. He was slapping peanut butter on his toast.

"I wonder if you can help me finish this crossword puzzle." Aunt Bets picked up a folded newspaper from the table. "I was doing it while I was waiting for you to come home. I adore crossword puzzles, but there's always one miserable word I can't get. What's a four-letter word for 'a tedious undertaking'? James doesn't seem to know."

Andrea looked at Jim, who was stuffing peanut butter and toast into his mouth. He looked back at her, swallowed, and silently mouthed the letters *B-E-T-S*.

Andrea started to giggle and then let out a long sigh left over from crying. "I guess I don't know, either."

"Never mind, I'll finish it later." Aunt Bets took a handbag from the window seat and put it on her arm. "I was just waiting for you to come home before I went to the market. You and James tell me what you'd like for our first dinner together, and that's what we'll have. What'll it be? James?"

"Doesn't matter." Jim sounded bored. He was carefully spreading peanut butter to all corners of his second piece of toast.

"Chicken soup and biscuits," said Andrea quickly. That was one of her favorite meals.

"Chicken soup and biscuits it is. I won't be long." Aunt Bets swept out the kitchen door, leaving a trail of cologne-scented air behind her.

Jim turned and looked at Andrea with an expression of complete disgust. His lips were pressed together so his chin jutted out like Aunt Bets's, and he was screwing the lid onto the peanut butter jar so hard that she wondered if it was going to shatter. She thought of the mournful little old lady she had imagined Aunt Bets to be, and she couldn't help grinning. "This is a good chance for us to get acquainted," she said brightly.

Jim stared at her. Then his mouth relaxed and a

gleam appeared in his eyes. "Right. First, I've got to tell you you'd look *so* much more youthful with just a touch of rouge on the cheekbones." He scooped a gob of peanut butter from the toast with his forefinger and reached out toward Andrea's face.

"Hey!" As she ducked away, laughing, some of the peanut butter got in her hair.

Jim was laughing, too. "Sport, we're in trouble. Can you believe Mother stuck us with this weird lady for six days? You should have been here when the United Parcel truck came. She introduced us and I had to shake hands with the guy—he just wanted to get out of here—and then she started going on to him about how I took after her side of the family. Oh, by the way, that's your package."

"Really?" Andrea looked again at the big package on the table. Who would be sending her a package, especially such a large one? Her birthday was in August. She lifted the carton from the table—it wasn't heavy—and looked at the return address. Aero-Joy Products, Inc. "Oh! It's the—it's the kit I sent away for."

"Kit for what?" Jim's voice was muffled with peanut butter and toast. "C'mon, open it, let's see how bad they gypped you." He reached for the package, but Andrea turned away, hugging it to her chest.

"Leave it alone, it's mine." She stacked the bird nest carton on top of the package and edged toward the door. "I'm going to open it in my room."

Jim shrugged and turned back to the toaster. "Have fun, sucker."

Up in her room Andrea knelt on the floor, carefully

cutting the taped ends of the package with her scissors. Her breath was short from excitement and from hurrying up the stairs. Jim might be right. Maybe she was a sucker to pay $5.98 for a wings kit. On the other hand, why would the advertisement say "money-back guarantee" if the wings didn't work?

Underneath the brown paper was a cardboard box, about the size of a box for boots. *WONDA-WINGS* it said on the top of the box in red letters. There were little wings on both *W*'s.

Andrea lifted off the lid. There was a plastic bag the size of a pillow filled with red, blue, and yellow feathers. There were also two folded pieces of pinkish material, a smaller plastic bag of sticklike things, a plastic bottle labeled *Aero-hesive,* and a glass bottle labeled *Aero-Joy Juice.* The spaces in the box were filled with what looked like birds' nests—fat coils of narrow, springy strips of wood.

Andrea stared doubtfully at the kit. Was this stuff really going to turn into wings? She hoped there were directions. Taking everything out of the box, she found a leaflet under the bottom layer of coiled shavings. She read, "Follow these directions for easy assembly.

"1. PINION-PELTS. Spread Auto-activating Pinion-Pelts on 4′ x 4′ flat surface (Fig. 1)."

Good grief. These were directions for grown-ups. But difficult directions were not going to stop her. She would look at them carefully, one bit at a time, the way she worked jigsaw puzzles. First, Fig. 1.

On the same page of the leaflet there was a picture

labeled *Fig. 1.* It showed two teardrop shapes spread out on a table. The teardrops must be the Auto-activating Pinion-Pelts. And there was only one thing in the box that could be—Andrea shook out one of the folded pieces. Yes, it was teardrop shaped, about the size of a dish towel. She shook out the other piece—it was just the same. She didn't have a big table, but she could spread them out on the floor if she rolled the braided rug back toward the bed.

Except the jigsaw puzzle she had just finished would be in the way. She looked at the puzzle, a scene of a young robin teetering on the edge of its nest while its parents fluttered anxiously around it. Five hundred pieces. It was a shame to take it apart. But there was nowhere else to put the wings together. Andrea quickly scooped the pieces into the puzzle box and shoved it onto the bottom shelf of the bookcase.

Then she spread out one of the pink Pinion-Pelts. The material felt like thin leather. It had long, narrow pockets in it that formed a sort of backwards *N* across the teardrop shape. Each pocket was marked with a number followed by the letter *R*. She picked up the other Pinion-Pelt and examined it. It had numbered pockets, too, but the letter was *L*. Right and left, they must mean.

The directions went on.

"2. Aero-Frame Support System. Matching numbers and letters, insert Aero-Frame units in Pinion-Pelt (Fig. 2)." There was another picture, Fig. 2. It showed sticks sliding into the pockets in the Pinion-Pelt. Oh, the bag of funny-shaped sticks.

Andrea took one stick out of the bag. It was much lighter than it looked. Let's see, this one was marked *3R*. She tried the stick in the 3R pocket. It slid in easily. What would keep it from sliding out?

Fig. 3, right beside Fig. 2, showed a bottle marked *Aero-hesive* dripping a drop into a pocket. The Aero-hesive bottle looked a lot like a bottle of Elmer's glue, but the sticky stuff that she squeezed out of the top was clear pink. And when she pressed the opening of the pocket together with the glue, it sealed as if it had grown together.

Once she got the hang of it, the rest of the sticks didn't take long. Then the directions went on.

"3. AERO-PLUME SYSTEM." This must be the feathers. Yes, it was. *Aero-Plumes,* the pillow-sized bag was marked. "Matching Aero-Plume colors to colors of Aero-Plume Follicles in Pinion-Pelt (Fig. 4)—" Thank goodness for pictures.

In Fig. 4 the Pinion-Pelts were divided into three parts. The top was labeled *red,* the middle *blue,* and the bottom *yellow.* A little feather was sticking out of the top, a medium-sized one out of the middle, and a big one out of the bottom. She looked from the picture to the pieces of material on the floor. They were covered with tiny dots, so faint she hadn't noticed them before. Red dots on top . . .

Andrea took a yellow feather from the bag and poked it at a yellow dot. It slipped into the material with a *thunk*ing sound, like a little cork fitting into a bottle.

That was the first yellow feather. There were

hundreds of them, but Andrea just kept poking them into the yellow dots, row after row. Then hundreds of blue feathers, row after row, and then hundreds of fluffy little red feathers. And then she had to turn the Pinion-Pelt over and do the same thing on the other side. As she worked she sucked the end of one pony-tail, the one Jim had accidentally smeared with peanut butter.

It took her a long time to cover one Pinion-Pelt completely with feathers. Almost completely, that is—there was a round blank spot on one side at the larger end. When she had finished, she stood up stiffly—her left foot had gone to sleep while she was working—and took a good look at it.

The sight made her catch her breath. It was the most beautiful thing she had ever seen. The feathers gleamed softly, not like dyed dime-store Indian head-dress feathers, but like part of a live bird.

It was hard to be patient now, she was so eager to finish the second wing. A couple of times she accidentally tried to stick a red feather into a blue dot, or a blue feather into a yellow dot, and almost bent the quill. But finally the second wing lay glowing on her bedroom floor beside the first.

The wings were not flat, but slightly cupped, curving from red to blue to yellow, with purple and green where the colors overlapped. They were so beautiful that Andrea almost forgot what they were supposed to be for and just admired them. Then she thought about how it would look if a bird were spreading these wings, and she felt sad. She hadn't been gypped exactly, but she didn't see how she could put the wings on even to pretend to fly. There weren't any straps or pins or other fasteners in the carton.

She picked up the directions and looked at them again. Oh, there was more on the back side.

"4. ATTACHMENT. Place assembled Wonda-Wings convex side down—" Fig. 5 was a picture of the wings side by side on the floor with the Aero-hesive bottle dripping onto a bare circle on one wing.

She turned the wings so that they cupped upward, as it showed in the picture. Toward the top inside edge of each wing there was a featherless space about as big as a pancake. So they glued on! She had wondered why the feathers didn't cover the whole Pinion-Pelt. She opened the Aero-hesive bottle again and squeezed clear pink goo over both circles, careful not to get it on the feathers. Now what?

"With shoulder blades bare, press back firmly against Wonda-Wings, making sure that Contact Points meet with shoulder blades (Fig. 6)." Fig. 6 was a stick person lying on top of a pair of wings. "Do not move Wonda-Wings until Aero-hesive has set (approx. 5 min.)."

Andrea hesitated a moment, her heart beating fast. Then she pulled off her T-shirt and lay carefully back onto the wings, looking over her shoulder to make sure she got the circles on her shoulder blades. The Aero-hesive made two cool, wet spots on her back.

Let's see, five minutes—rats. She should have placed the wings so she could see the clock on her night table.

The clock was on the other side of the bed, and she was afraid to disturb the glue. She would just have to count out the seconds, five times sixty. Well, if she had the patience to poke thousands of feathers into the Pinion-Pelts, she certainly had the patience to count three hundred seconds. She began counting firmly. "One, two, three, four, five." Looking at the window, she noticed clouds in the sky had turned pink, reflecting the sunset. How long had she been working up here?

"Andrea!" Aunt Bets's voice called musically up the staircase. "Dinnertime!"

"I'm coming!" It was hard to shout lying on her back. "Six, seven, eight . . ." As Andrea counted she noticed a thick coil of the wood strips from the Wonda-Wings carton on the floor near her face. It looked a lot like a bird's nest. She wondered if there was some purpose to these coils besides stuffing up the carton. The directions hadn't said anything about them.

When Andrea had counted three minutes and twenty-one seconds she heard the second call. Even two floors away she could tell Aunt Bets was a little irritated.

"Coming right away!" Andrea couldn't think of an excuse. She couldn't shout "I'm in the bathroom" because there was no bathroom on this floor.

Forty seconds later footsteps pounded up the stairs and a fist thumped on the door. Jim's voice growled, "Andrea, c'mon, for pete's sake. She won't let me eat until you get down there, and I'm starved."

"I'm coming," yelled Andrea. "I'm coming!" She was almost finished. "Fifty-nine, sixty—five minutes." She sat up cautiously. With a soft rustle the wings came too. They were stuck tight. They were going to stay on!

Andrea scrambled to her feet. Then she glanced over her shoulder at the mirror. The wings looked great, but she needed something to cover them up, quickly. She ran to the closet, yanked her bathrobe from a hook, and hurried to the door buttoning it.

She opened the door. Jim was standing there with his hands on his hips. "About time." He clattered down the stairs in front of her.

Aunt Bets was sitting at the kitchen table, waiting for Andrea to slide into her chair. "Now that we are all here, the hostess will lift her soup spoon, and everyone may eat." She picked up her spoon. "Andrea, do you generally wear your bathrobe to the dinner table?"

"Oh, no." Andrea laughed and shrugged as if she could understand why Aunt Bets was puzzled. "I was just sort of tired, and I thought I'd start getting ready for bed early." She smiled brightly at her great-aunt and picked up her own spoon.

Jim silently took three biscuits and popped them into his mouth one after the other, as if they had been peanuts. It must be hard to be so big, thought Andrea. He has to eat all the time just to keep alive. Those hormones, making him grow. He can't help it.

Andrea was hungry herself, after going without any afternoon snack, and after all that crying and all that work. Three things that always made her hungry. But nothing tasted quite right. When she had told Aunt Bets she wanted chicken soup and biscuits, she had really meant Mother's chicken soup and biscuits. She swallowed the lump of food in her mouth, feeling a pang of loneliness. She leaned back against her chair, and then straightened up quickly. The wings. She didn't want to crush the feathers.

"I see I haven't lost my touch with biscuits," said Aunt Bets pleasantly, buttering one for herself. "*Or* chicken soup. As my cousin Clara used to say, if you want to make good chicken soup, you have to put your heart into it. Now, how about a quiz question for the two of you, from my crossword puzzle? Packing material, nine letters, second letter *x*? I'll even give you a hint: 'A banner with the strange device—' It's the last word of that line. Of course that helps Jim more than Andrea, since he's surely read that poem in his English class."

"I surely never heard that poem in my life." Jim was finally irritated enough to speak. He ladled soup into his mouth and wiped his chin with his napkin.

"Maybe it's considered old-fashioned now." Aunt Bets smiled at Andrea. "Very well, here's another hint: it's Latin for 'higher.' James, don't tell me you've never taken Latin!"

Jim shrugged and drained the last drops of soup from his bowl. "Okay, I won't tell you." He gulped down his milk. "Excuse me."

"Yes, you may be excused, James. Don't feel bad that you couldn't answer the question. You've set a new record for speed-eating."

Jim grinned grudgingly at the floor as he pushed back his chair. "It tasted good. Thanks."

Andrea was amazed to hear Jim say that. Maybe he was so hungry he couldn't tell the difference. Then she remembered the question. "What's the answer, Aunt Bets? I don't know Latin either."

"Excelsior." Aunt Bets's brown eyes shone under her purplish eye shadow as she recited at Jim's departing back,

> "Try not the Pass!" the old man said;
> "Dark lowers the tempest overhead,
> The roaring torrent is deep and wide!"
> And loud that clarion voice replied,
>   Excelsior!
>   —Henry Wadsworth Longfellow

Andrea liked the way Aunt Bets rolled the *r* at the end of *Excelsior*. But there was something bothering her. "Wait a minute. I thought you said the word in the crossword puzzle meant 'packing material.' "

"Absolutely right." Aunt Bets beamed at her. "Aren't you on the ball! That's another meaning. Do you know what excelsior is? I don't think they use it much anymore, with this new Styrofoam stuff. It's like long thin wood shavings."

"Oh." Andrea remembered the coils of wood strips in the Wonda-Wings carton. "I guess I have seen it. It looks like birds' nests?"

"Mm, I suppose maybe it does. I haven't seen many birds' nests. Isn't it funny they called it 'excelsior'? I don't see any connection between shavings and *higher*."

33

Andrea was glad to know the excelsior was just packing material. As she climbed the stairs to her room after dinner she practiced rolling her *r*'s: "Excelsior. Excelsiorrr!"

~~ **3** ~~

Excelsiorrr!

Andrea shut the door to her room and carefully slid out of her bathrobe, wincing as some of the feathers bent the wrong way. She turned her back to the mirror above her dresser and twisted her neck to see if the wings had been damaged.

They were gorgeous, still glowing red, blue, and yellow, and all the colors of the rainbow where the feathers overlapped. But they hung limply down her back like two big feather dusters. They were not, of course, real wings. She jumped up and down and wiggled her shoulder blades—nothing. She stood on the edge of her bed and leaped, flapping her arms. The wings lifted briefly, tugging her upwards a little, and then fell softly against her back as her feet touched the floor.

Andrea hadn't really believed that she would be able to fly with the wings. After all, she was nine, not three.

Just the same, she felt disappointed. She decided to take them off and go downstairs to watch TV until bedtime.

But when she reached behind her and tugged at the wings where they joined her back, they wouldn't come off. She pulled harder, hoping she wouldn't tear the wings—ouch! It seemed more likely that she would tear her back. It felt worse than trying to pull off a Band-Aid stuck to a scab.

Andrea pulled and pried and jerked at the wings, getting more and more worried. Then she remembered the directions and looked at them again. But she couldn't find any mention of how to get unstuck from the Wonda-Wings. The only thing in the directions she hadn't read before was the very last sentence.

"5. ACTIVATION. Ingest Aero-Joy Juice."

Andrea picked the Aero-Joy Juice bottle out of a pile of excelsior coils. It was about the size of a pint jar of pickles. The liquid inside it was pink. She unscrewed the cap and sniffed. Smelled like Hawaiian Punch.

The directions seemed to mean that she was supposed to drink the Aero-Joy Juice. But should she? This mysterious bottle seemed like the kind of thing her mother had always warned her against. No, thanks. She put the bottle down.

But Andrea still didn't know how to get the wings off. Maybe if she rubbed the wings really hard, instead of pulling at them . . . She threw herself on the floor and squirmed around on her back like a dog. Then she stood up and looked hopefully in the mirror, tugging at the wings. The feathers were a little rumpled, but the wings were still firmly attached.

Andrea needed help. If Mother were here . . . She wasn't. There were Aunt Bets and Jim. Aunt Bets was sort of interesting, but Andrea didn't think she could trust her. She didn't seem to have common sense about some things, like whether Jim would enjoy guessing games that required him to remember old-fashioned poems. And Andrea was afraid Aunt Bets would think she was babyish for sending away for the wings. How embarrassing.

Jim already thought she was a sucker, even though he didn't know it was wings she'd sent away for. She had nothing to lose with him. She put on her pajamas and bathrobe and went downstairs to find her brother.

Andrea found him in the family room, sprawled on the sofa with one eye on the TV and one eye on his homework.

"Jim," she whispered, walking up to the sofa.

"Hey, move it, sport." Jim waved her aside, still look-ing at the screen. "What?"

Andrea obediently moved from in front of the TV. "Jim, you know that thing I sent away for with the money order? Well, it was a kit for wings." She paused and braced herself.

"Wings?" Jim was so astonished that he jerked his eyes from the TV to her. "What do you mean, wings?"

Andrea felt her face getting red. "Wings, like wings to fly with. With feathers, like bird wings. I glued them on my back and now I can't get them off."

Jim stared at her without saying anything. Then he blinked. "You're kidding me. Wings to fly with? You really thought you could put these wings together and stick them on your back and fly with them? How old are you, anyway? Nine? Hey, did you ever hear that people can't fly? Come on!"

"I know, I know." Andrea had expected this, but she hated to hear it anyway. "But will you help me get them off?"

Jim shifted the textbook on his stomach, but he didn't sit up. "Why don't you get Aunt Bets to help you?" There was a sarcastic tone in his voice. "She knows everything."

"I don't want to ask Aunt Bets," said Andrea stubbornly. She picked at the lint in her bathrobe pocket and wondered how to persuade him. Then she had an inspiration. "I just thought you could do it better."

Jim looked surprised, then a little embarrassed. He put his book facedown on the floor and slowly sat up. "Well—all right, I'll do it for you. Turn around."

"Okay, but be careful." Andrea squirmed out of her bathrobe and turned around. "Oww!" Jim had grabbed one wing under her pajama top and jerked sharply.

"Jeez!" He hastily let go. "Keep it down! You'd think I was killing you."

"It hurt!" she gasped. "The glue's really stuck." They both listened for Aunt Bets, who must have heard that scream. But the only sounds from the kitchen were the throb and splash of the dishwasher and the clanking of pans.

They sighed with relief. Then Andrea whispered, "What am I going to do?"

"Well—" Jim looked as if he was losing interest in her problem. "I'd say take a hot bath and soak your back, and let it alone overnight. I bet when you get up tomorrow they'll fall off." He put his feet back up on the sofa and opened his book again.

Lying in a hot tub made Andrea sleepy, and drying the wings with Jim's hair dryer seemed to take forever. Then she had to kiss Aunt Bets good-night and climb all the way upstairs. At last she was about to crawl into bed, very tired—and realized she was also very thirsty. She had forgotten to get a drink of water before she came up to her room. Was she thirsty enough to go down to the bathroom again?

Then her eye fell on the bottle of Aero-Joy Juice beside the empty Wonda-Wings carton. She loved Hawaiian Punch. Wouldn't it be silly not to drink it, if that's what it was? She picked up the bottle and looked at the label.

AERO-JOY JUICE
Drink to activate Wonda-Wings*

At the bottom of the label it said, in tiny letters:

*Contains avesin, an experimental hormone preparation. To be ingested only by persons intending to develop pectoral and dorsal flight musculature.

That didn't sound so bad. The juice wasn't poison. There was nothing wrong with developing muscles.

And it seemed to have to do with making the wings work.

But she was trying to get the wings off.

But if they worked, she wouldn't want to take them off. Either way, it would be all right. And her throat was so dry.

Andrea hesitated, then put the bottle to her lips and sipped. Yep, Hawaiian Punch. *Glug-glug-glug.*

She put the bottle down, looked in the mirror again and wiggled her shoulder blades. How silly. How could Hawaiian Punch make her fly? She climbed into bed.

Andrea rolled over on her back, the way she always did to go to sleep, but now the bony parts of the wings stuck knobbily into her shoulders. It was not comfortable. She turned onto her stomach, pressing her cheek against the pillow. That position felt odd. She wondered if she could get to sleep this way. . . .

Late that night, when the house was still and the moon was shining in Andrea's window, she dreamed that a mosquito was biting her back. Only it wasn't exactly a mosquito, because the two itching spots on her back were really tingling more than itching. Like the way her foot had felt that afternoon when she sat on it and it went to sleep. The mosquito must be huge, because she could hear its wings whirring above her as she lay on her stomach—

Andrea was wide-awake, as if a light switch had turned on in her brain. She was lying facedown, as in the dream, but her stomach was not pressing against the bed. Her cheek was not on her pillow. Her pajama

41

top was pushed up under her arms, instead of covering her chest and back.

Andrea opened her eyes. A square of moonlight lay on her rumpled sheets and blanket, two feet below her.

The wings flapping above her, loud as the wings of a startled goose, were her own.

In her amazement Andrea stopped flapping, and plopped onto her bed. For a moment she thought she must have been dreaming the whole thing. She jumped out of bed and peered into the dark mirror over her dresser, trying to spread the wings.

They didn't spread, but she thought she felt a new kind of twitch in her back. She tried again, her heart pounding. This time she moved only her shoulder blades.

Andrea blew out her breath and stamped her feet impatiently. They had to work. She knew they worked—hadn't she been hovering over her bed in her sleep? She made herself stand still and concentrated as hard as she could on spreading the wings.

There! She felt a strange pulling under the skin of her chest and back. The wings stretched out awkwardly, the right one farther than the left. She tried to fold them, but they wouldn't go back exactly flat. Then she tried to spread them again, and with a sudden rush of air they opened all the way out.

She gasped. Their colors were gray in the dim mirror, but there they were, reaching way out on either side. She tried to fold them. They disappeared behind her back.

Was it a dream, after all? Andrea felt the cool wood

of the floor under her feet. There was her familiar hairbrush on the dresser. She was not dreaming—the wings were working!

With mounting excitement she climbed onto the headboard of her bed. "Excelsior!" Opening the wings, Andrea leaped off the headboard. She sailed across the room and crashed into the bookcase. It teetered, and a pile of comic books slithered to the floor. Andrea ran back to the bed.

"Excelsiorrr!" Again she jumped and sailed, this time slamming into the wall beside the bookcase. Flying, flying, she was flying! She breathed in deep, joyous breaths, and the air filled her chest as if she were a balloon. Flying! She felt dizzy.

Over and over again Andrea climbed onto the headboard, and over and over she whooshed the length of the room. Her shoulder should have been aching from banging against the wall, but she felt nothing except overwhelming delight. She half expected to break through the wall as if it were cardboard and burst out into the sky.

Out into the sky. Yes. Andrea picked herself up from her last crash landing and looked out the window. The scene outside, lit by the full moon, seemed like a different world. There was the lawn and the hedge and the driveway and the big maple tree, just as usual, but so different.

It was the colors. They weren't the regular nighttime black and gray. The grass was almost green. The leaves on the maple tree were almost red. She looked down at her hand, almost pink. This was a world in which anything could happen. A world in which Andrea could jump off the roof and fly all the way to the maple tree.

Andrea pushed up the window, then the screen. As she stepped out onto the gritty asphalt shingles she saw the round moon itself high over the maple tree. The sky around it was almost blue.

On her hands and knees she clambered past the window to the peak of the roof and crawled along to where the house met the garage. It wasn't much of a drop to the garage roof. She stood up, spread her wings, and—before she could think it over—jumped.

The wings pulled Andrea up and held. She was airborne. She was gliding on the night breeze as if she were floating down a river. She felt a rush of joy. She wanted to shout, "Look! It's me, Andrea! Flying!"

Then Andrea looked down and saw the edge of the garage roof and the basketball net slip under her dangling feet. She felt her wings start to fold. For a terrified instant she hung in the air, staring at the hard pavement of the driveway fifteen feet below.

Then she pulled down with her wings . . . and pulled them up again . . . and felt herself surging forward. The wings flapped steadily, powerfully, and she was not falling. She was rising slightly as she zoomed straight toward the maple tree.

Stop! Turn! She couldn't stop or turn.

"Unhh!" Andrea put out her hands to grab a branch, but still she thudded against the tree trunk so hard that her breath came out all at once. "Ow!" Clinging to the branch with her feet swinging far above the ground, she hoped that she really was dreaming and now she would wake up safe in bed. But the chilly night breeze kept on blowing up her pajama legs and her shoulder throbbed. She hauled herself up to sit on the branch.

Shivering, Andrea looked at her smarting hands. She had scraped them hard on the bark of the tree. She could see drops of almost-red blood.

Now what? She couldn't climb down the tree, because this was the lowest branch. And she certainly didn't want to sit up here like a stranded kitten until morning, when Aunt Bets and Jim would wake up.

She could jump off the branch and glide to the ground. But then she would still be outside, and Aunt Bets would have locked the doors.

"Hoo-hoo," said a voice behind Andrea, so close that she almost fell off the branch. What was that? Something right there in the tree with her.

In the mottled moonlight coming through the maple leaves it was hard to see the owl at first. Andrea saw the eyes blink, and the speckled feathers ruffle and settle down again. She wondered why the owl was so angry at her. . . .

She knew what the owl was thinking! How could she? She wasn't reading its mind exactly—it was more like understanding the expression on someone's face. "*My* mice," the owl seemed to say. "Go away!"

It would have been funny if the owl hadn't been so big, and if its thoughts hadn't been so harsh. Andrea saw its beak open and close with a snap, as if it were digging into a mouse's soft body. She looked around uneasily. Now this almost-colored shadowy world seemed menacing. She wanted to go back to her bedroom.

She had to fly back to the roof, and the power and joy seemed to have leaked out of her like air out of a balloon. She glanced at the owl. It shifted its feet a little way down the branch and then back again. The moonlight glinted from its eyes. She wanted to get away from it.

Andrea couldn't stand it any longer. She shoved herself into the air above the driveway.

Flap, flap, flap. She was afraid of crashing into the house the way she had crashed into the maple tree, but this time she managed to beat her wings more slowly and land softly on the shingles in front of her window. She grabbed the sill and crawled over it.

Safe inside. She turned and looked out toward the maple tree. The owl was still sitting on the same branch, a dark hunched shape, waiting. As she stared at it, hugging herself against the chill, it let out a long, low hoot. Andrea jumped into bed and pulled up the covers.

4

I Can Fly

Andrea opened her eyes to clear, bright October daylight. For a moment she couldn't remember what was so wonderful, and then it came back to her. "I can fly!" She leaped out of bed, sprang into the air, and sailed the length of the room. She didn't crash into the wall this time, but as she landed gently with her hands on the bookcase she remembered her scraped palms. "Ow!" It had happened, all right.

She had to tell Jim. She pulled on her jeans and a T-shirt, easing the shirt carefully over the wings, and ran out of the room.

Jim was in the bathroom on the second floor, shaving. He frowned at her in the mirror as she burst through the half-open door. "Hey, watch it. You almost made me cut myself."

"Jim, guess what!"

He glanced down at her sideways as he scraped the shaving cream from his chin. "What—did the wings come off? I knew—"

"I can fly!" She leaned toward him, gripping the edge of the counter with her fingers. "I woke up last night and the wings were working. I flew around the bedroom and then I flew out the window, all the way to the tree at the end of the driveway." She paused and shuddered. "There was an owl there and he was pretty mean-looking, so I flew back to my room." She looked at him expectantly.

"Well—that's a pretty interesting dream, I guess." Jim rinsed his razor under the faucet. "Hey, are you the one who clogged up my hair dryer with fluff? I tried to use it this morning and the motor burned out." He pointed to the hair dryer, which was lying on the floor with its cord curling behind the toilet. Andrea noticed for the first time a funny smell in the air. Burned feathers.

"Oh, I'm sorry. I had to dry the wings before I went to bed. But it wasn't a dream! Look—I scraped up my hands when I bumped into the tree." She held up her palms.

Jim, who had started to shave again, glanced at her hands. He whistled and put the razor down. "Man, you did a job on them. Better go ask Aunt Bets to put Band-Aids on your hands."

"Okay." Andrea started to go out the door. Then she stopped.

"Well, go on." Jim looked at her out of the corner of his eye, with his chin tilted up to shave its underside.

49

"Why can't you do it? I don't want to tell Aunt Bets about flying." She smiled at him and blinked her eyes. "Besides, you took first aid."

Jim shook his head. "Jeez. You don't have to take first aid to put a Band-Aid on someone." But he looked pleased. "All right, just a second. I've got to finish shaving."

He drew the razor over the last few patches of stubble, rinsed his face, and rubbed it with a towel. Then he took the Band-Aid box from the medicine cabinet. "Wash your hands."

Andrea gingerly washed her hands.

"Now hold them out—whoops."

The largest Band-Aid was much too small for the scrapes on Andrea's palms.

"I guess I need the first-aid kit after all."

The first-aid kit was in the cupboard under the sink. Jim found a tube of ointment, which he spread on the scrapes, and a gauze pad to tape over each palm. "What're you going to tell Aunt Bets, if you aren't going to tell her about flying? She'll still wonder what happened to your hands."

Jim was right. Andrea thought a moment. "I'll just say I got up early and did too many handstands and got blisters."

Jim looked at her, smiling. "Handstands, huh? You nutty kid." He punched her shoulder lightly.

"Ow!" Andrea flinched. "That's my bruise. Where I crashed into the wall last night."

Jim seemed surprised. "Sorry." Then he smiled again. "You can tell Aunt Bets you fell over doing

handstands and hit your shoulder against the bookcase."

Andrea nodded thoughtfully. "Hey, that's a good
idea. I will tell her that."

"I guess you've got it all figured out, then. Except
for one thing—you can't wear those wings to school. I
can see them sticking out under your shirt."

Andrea went back to her room and looked over her
shoulder into the mirror. Jim was right again. They
did stick out below her T-shirt. Not only that, they
made bulges under the shirt. The folded wings fit
closely to her body, but anyone could tell there was
something there. She couldn't wear her bathrobe to
school. What else could she wear that was thick, that
would cover her whole back?

On the shelf of her closet she found a hooded white
cable-knit sweater that Mother had been saving for her
to wear next year. With the wings it fit just about right,
although she had to turn back the cuffs. Andrea
checked in the mirror as she buttoned it up. Yes, that
would do. The thick sweater came down over her hips,
covering the wings with a couple of inches to spare.
And the hood hanging from the back of the neck
helped conceal the bulges.

At breakfast Aunt Bets *tsk-tsk*ed over Andrea's
hands, but she didn't seem to notice anything strange
about her back. "Isn't that a pretty sweater on you, darling. It sets off your dark hair so nicely. Looks like it's
hand-knit, too."

Andrea rode her bike to school, sweating a little because it was warm for October. But she thought she'd sweat a lot more if Julie or Scott saw the wings under her T-shirt. In the classroom she took a piece of paper and began to copy the spelling words from the chalkboard.

"What's the matter with your hands?" Lauren was sliding into the seat next to Andrea as if she had never laughed at her.

Andrea hadn't really forgiven Lauren for that, but she let her peek under one of the gauze pads.

"I got blisters on my hands once from swinging on the bars," said Lauren. "Worse sores than that."

It was Friday, a geography day. "And this week, boys and girls, we're going to begin an exciting new project," said Miss Silvano.

Andrea glanced at Lauren, who was gazing doubtfully at the teacher. Lauren must be thinking the same thing she was thinking—that they weren't always excited by what Miss Silvano said was exciting.

"Now we've spent the last week learning about someone who took a very famous trip. His name is—" Miss Silvano paused.

Andrea thought Miss Silvano really should be teaching kindergarten instead of fourth grade, but she chorused with the rest of the class, "Columbus."

"Right." Miss Silvano smiled at them. "Now each one of us is going to plan his or her own special trip."

Lauren glanced at Andrea and raised her eyebrows. Andrea raised hers back. Maybe this project would be fun, after all.

"We'll spend some time this afternoon looking at the

globe and the atlas and these *National Geographic* magazines I brought in, and we'll think about it over the weekend. Then Monday I want each of you to choose a place you'd like to go to, and start working on a diary—what you imagine your trip would be like."

"I'm going to Zambia to hunt elephants!" called out Scott.

"I'm going to Acapulco!" said Julie.

Everyone started to talk at once, but somehow when Andrea blurted out, "I'm going to fly south with the geese," there was complete silence. They looked at her. Julie giggled, and Scott made a noise like a honking goose.

"I mean—to Florida," said Andrea.

"That's a very imaginative trip, Andrea," said Miss Silvano. "All you need is a pair of wings!"

At recess that afternoon Andrea climbed to the top of the jungle gym and sat there, looking out over the playground. All the other girls were playing kickball, but she didn't feel like it. She could fly. She wished she could pull off her sweater now and leap into the sky, high above the screaming kickball players and even above the soaring kickball.

But she would have to wait until she got home this afternoon to fly. Right now she would just sit on top of the jungle gym and remember how she had jumped from the roof into the night breeze, and how her strong, beautiful wings had saved her from crashing on the driveway and carried her all the way to the maple tree.

"Andrea." Miss Silvano, who had playground duty, paused beside the jungle gym. "Andrea, wouldn't you like to join in the kickball game? I'm sure Julie could use a good kicker like you on her team."

"No, I guess not." I'm sure Julie could use a good kick in the pants, thought Andrea.

Miss Silvano did not move on. "I don't think you need such a heavy sweater on a nice day like this, do you?" She stretched out her hand. "I'll hold it for you until after recess, if you like, so it won't get dirty."

"No, thank you." Andrea thought about how itchy and sweaty she felt around her neck. She also noticed the teacher looked a little worried. Miss Silvano thought there was something wrong with her. With an effort Andrea smiled cheerfully and said, "You see, it's very breezy up here."

"Oh, I see." Miss Silvano still looked puzzled. But she strolled away, fingering the whistle hanging from a chain around her neck.

After school, just as Andrea was backing her bicycle out of the bike rack, she heard Lauren calling her name. She turned and waited as Lauren came running up. "What do you want?"

Lauren's round face was flushed from hurrying, and she had to pause a moment before she could stop panting and speak. "Can you come over this afternoon?"

Andrea hesitated. Then she remembered again how Lauren had laughed yesterday while Julie made fun of her. Besides, she wanted to get home and fly. "I don't really feel like it today." She threw her leg over the

bike. " 'Bye." She turned away from Lauren's hurt expression and pedaled off down the street.

At home Andrea hurried up the stairs, wiggling out of her big sweater. In her room she took off her T-shirt, too, and put on a halter top that left her wings free. There! She was ready to fly.

Then she paused at the door of her room. Where could she fly? She had planned to go into the backyard, but Aunt Bets might look out the window and see her. If she didn't, that nosy neighbor who was always puttering around in her garden probably would, and she would call Aunt Bets.

Andrea went back in her room and shut the door. She would just practice flying in here for a while.

So she glided from the bed to the end of the room several times, but it wasn't as exciting as it had been last night. It wasn't real flying. If she flapped her wings at all, she would crash into the wall so hard she'd probably knock herself out, the way birds did on glass doors and windows.

Andrea floated gently to the floor one more time and sighed. She had to think of a good secret place to fly. She put on her sweater again and went slowly down the stairs.

At the bottom of the first flight she heard grunting and puffing noises from Jim's open door. He was doing push-ups. She leaned against the doorframe and watched him.

"Twenty-one . . ." He glanced up at her. "How's it going, sport?"

"Okay." She watched him lower himself to the floor

56

and then miraculously rise onto his palms and toes again. Push-ups were hard. She had tried them. "I have to find a good place to fly, though. My room is too small."

"Twenty-two . . . Why don't you"—he gasped for breath—"fly in the backyard?" Down to the floor again.

"No! Aunt Bets might see me there."

"Twenty-three . . . So what?"

Andrea was surprised she had to explain this to him. "She wouldn't let me do it. She'd think it was dangerous." She thought for a moment. "Actually I guess it is a little dangerous."

Jim nodded as he hoisted his body off the floor again. "Twenty-four . . . Parents . . . and people like that . . . think everything's dangerous."

Andrea squatted down on the floor near his head. It seemed strange, but really nice, to be talking to her brother as if he were a friend. She would add a big brother to her paper doll family. "Maybe I'll just have to fly outside at night when everyone's asleep, like I did last night."

Jim looked up at her sharply. "That's a dumb idea. . . . Twenty-five." He collapsed on the floor and blew out his breath. "Man, am I out of shape. —Listen, you better not let me catch you playing with your wings outside at night. There's lots of places you can go in the daytime where nobody would see you—what about the bird sanctuary?"

Andrea pictured herself soaring through the sky over the woods and pond and marsh. "That's a great idea!" Then she imagined a tiny person far below, pointing up at her and shouting. "But people take walks there sometimes. They'd see me."

Jim rested his chin on his arms. "Not if you fly in the woods."

She thought it over and nodded. "That really is a good idea. I like to go to the bird sanctuary anyway. Thanks."

Jim smiled an unexpectedly nice smile at her. "Anytime. Bring all your problems to James Reve. Fees reasonable."

≈ 5 ≈

A Good Place
for Flying

Aunt Bets, dressed in a Japanese kimono, dropped pancake batter onto the griddle. "Isn't it a beautiful day! Just like yesterday. What a gorgeous time of year to be in the country. I think I'll go to that barn sale on Heron Pond Lane—they advertised antiques. How about you, Andrea?"

"I'm going to go to the bird sanctuary and watch birds there. Mother lets me take my lunch and stay all day." It was almost true, although Mother had never let her go off by herself that long. Andrea looked sideways at Aunt Bets.

"Splendid! A splendid day for bird-watching. You plan to give us a full report at dinnertime." Aunt Bets put a plate of pancakes in front of Andrea. "Keep up your strength!"

Andrea wasn't usually very hungry for breakfast, but

59

today she felt she could eat the whole batch of pancakes. Until she took the first bite. "These pancakes taste sort of . . . different, Aunt Bets."

"Yes! How observant you are." Her great-aunt beamed at her. "It's my own secret ingredient"—she lowered her voice—"a pinch of cardamom."

Andrea didn't know what to say, so she took another bite. She had to eat them. She was starving. They didn't taste terrible exactly, just strange. Finally she drenched them with syrup and managed to eat the whole plateful.

Then she made two tuna salad sandwiches with plenty of pickles and celery and put them in a bag with an apple and a can of lemon soda. At least her lunch would taste the way it should.

Aunt Bets, eating her own pancakes, gazed out the bay window. "Such a lovely warm day." She looked back at Andrea. "Do you think you really need that heavy sweater, darling?"

Good grief. Just like Miss Silvano. Andrea shrugged and looked at Aunt Bets with innocent eyes. "It feels fine right now. If I get too warm later, I'll take it off."

"Well, it *is* becoming on you. Are you going? Have a lovely day!"

As Andrea wheeled her bike down the driveway she waved at Jim, who was pushing a sputtering lawn mower over the neighbors' grass. He waved back and wiped sweat off his forehead. It certainly was a warm day.

But Andrea was glad for that, because the halter top

was her only piece of clothing that left her wings free for flying. She needed to figure out something else for cool weather.

As she sped along Cross Street past the glowing red orange sumac bushes, the breeze lifted Andrea's ponytails. It was a little like flying. She took deep breaths, feeling lighter and lighter.

Here was the bird sanctuary, its fence almost hidden by wild grape vines. Their leaves had been yellow last week, but now they were brown and shriveled. Andrea sniffed the winy scent of fallen grapes as she parked her bike on the grass outside the gate.

Inside the fence was a pond running into an overgrown cranberry bog, edged by woods. On the far side of the pond ducks and geese floated through the reflections of trees. The geese weren't fat gray or white barnyard geese, but wild Canada geese with black white-cheeked heads and long, proud necks. Andrea counted fourteen of them—it must be the same flock that had been here since spring. Nine adults, two parents, and three goslings.

Andrea especially loved to watch the geese, but not right now. Now—her heart leaped—she was going to fly. She tossed her sweater and lunch bag at the foot of a spruce tree and ducked under its branches.

Among the pines and oaks and occasional beeches the sunlight was dimmer and the air still. A squirrel was chattering somewhere. Andrea looked up through feathery pine branches and dark red oak leaves to glimpses of the blue sky, and sighed happily. She had looked up like this many times, but never thinking that she could fly to the tops of those trees.

At the edge of a small clearing Andrea made a running start and jumped into the air, flapping her wings. She flew straight into a net of catbrier, scratching her arms and face, and dropped back to the ground. Ouch. That was the wrong direction to fly in.

She ran back across the clearing and jumped and flapped again, in a direction where the woods seemed free of catbrier. They weren't free of trees, though. Andrea flew smack into one, the way she had flown into the maple tree the other night, scraping her knee and dropping clumsily to the ground again. Oof. She couldn't seem to steer herself away from all these obstacles. It was like when she was learning to ride her bike and kept running into hedges and curbs.

Andrea picked her way through the catbrier to the edge of the woods and peered out. Could she risk flying in the open? She'd have to, or else she'd just be one big sore pretty soon. Anyway, there wasn't anyone around. It was worth the risk.

She stepped into the sunlight and started to run along the path like an airplane taking off. Flap, flap, flap. Jump! Andrea was sailing clear and free with her arms and legs stretched out, feeling muscles tug in her chest and back as the wings beat up and down. Hooray! Hooray! She laughed out loud.

Now she was skimming the yellow-leaved birches leaning over the pond. Now she was flying above the fire-colored blueberry bushes and burst-open cattails in

the bog. Uh-oh. If she kept on flying straight, she would crash into the woods on the other side of the marsh. She must be able to turn—after all, the birds did it.

She tried moving her body and arms and legs this way and that. There, that was it—she was leaning right, toward the pond, and she was turning back that way. And if she bent her knees she could move her feet like a tiller and turn even faster.

Andrea was so pleased that she swerved over the pond and past the path and circled out over the bog again. Then she turned back the other way, making a figure eight in the air.

As she brushed against a birch tree a red-winged blackbird flew up, squawking and flashing its color patches. It landed on a bush a few yards away and looked at her with its head to one side. "Danger?" it was asking itself. "No danger. Big clumsy pheasant."

Andrea let herself glide to a stop on the path and stared back at the blackbird. She knew what it was thinking, just the way she had known what the owl was thinking Thursday night. She suddenly understood a secret language.

"Food," thought the blackbird. "Back to flock." It flew across the pond to a large oak tree dotted with hundreds of blackbirds.

Andrea looked after it wonderingly for a moment, then shook her head and flapped up into the air herself. She wanted to figure out how to stop. She could stop by flying along the path more and more slowly and lower and lower until her feet touched the ground, but that wasn't good enough. She couldn't land on a branch that way, for instance.

After some experimenting, including a frightening moment when she turned a somersault and almost dropped into the pond, she had it. Stand up in the air, instead of lying down on it, and beat your wings backwards. Andrea flew triumphantly to the nearest pine tree and landed on a branch with a flourish of beating wings. A pair of mourning doves on a higher branch fluttered farther into the woods, twittering with surprise. "Geese in pines?" they seemed to ask each other.

"I'm not a goose," called Andrea. If she could understand the birds, maybe they could understand her. "I'm a flying girl!" But the mourning doves were gone.

Andrea shrugged and flew away from the pine tree. The important thing was, she could fly! She could turn, she could even stop short in the air. She had also figured how to go up or down—that was just a matter of tipping her body and the front edges of her wings.

Andrea swooped around the pond, past the dark red-leaved oak tree that the blackbirds had taken over. They filled the air with their squawks as they rose a few feet into the air, sank down again, and rose again, over and over. Their simple thoughts were mostly a kind of itchiness, a restlessness that rippled through the flock.

Sensing other thoughts from the pond, Andrea looked down. The geese were paddling along the edge of the water, dipping their long black necks beneath the surface. The itchy feeling came even more strongly from them. There was something they were supposed to be doing, but they weren't quite sure what it was yet.

The restlessness seemed catching. Andrea thought of something she wanted to do herself. She wanted to fly right up into the sky as far as she could go. She couldn't go straight up, like a rocket, but she began to circle the pond in a rising spiral, around and around, up, up, up. The pond shrank to the size of a mirror set among twig trees. She could see the red orange sumac bushes along Cross Street, and the houses half hidden by trees near the bird sanctuary.

Andrea circled higher and higher. She felt dizzy with happiness. The landscape below had spread out to include more houses, more crisscrossing roads with an occasional toylike car crawling along. Andrea was reminded of the relief map of Rushfield displayed in the school library, only this scene showed every little alley and vegetable garden.

Then without warning Andrea's breath was torn from her mouth. Gasping, she struggled to right herself. Something invisible but very strong was shoving against her face and chest, twisting her wings. Wind! She had flown into a river of wind.

Now she was sailing with the current, no longer tumbled around—but where was she going? She couldn't recognize Rushfield anywhere below. Little houses and stores, connected by a web of roads, stretched on and on. In one direction stacks of puffy clouds rested on the horizon. In the other a cluster of tiny skyscrapers perched at the edge of the flat ocean. For a sickening moment Andrea felt like a winged giant who could never possibly fit back into that miniature landscape.

Unnerved, Andrea folded her wings and dropped out of the wind current. Help! Flapping furiously, she pulled herself out of a nose dive. Stay calm. All she had to do was spiral down slowly the way she had flown up. But which of those blue spots below was the bird sanctuary pond? Maybe the wind had carried her so far that she wouldn't be able to find her way back.

But as Andrea flew in wider and lower circles she glimpsed a marsh grooved with drainage ditches beside one of the ponds. That looked right. Swerving toward it, she saw the gate and her bicycle, and sighed with relief. The ducks and geese fluttered on the water as she flew over the pond.

Andrea suddenly felt tired. She circled the pond one last time and came to rest on the path by the edge of the water. That had been frightening, being caught in the wind. She would have to be careful.

Then Andrea saw the geese paddling toward her, doubling up their necks every few seconds. She looked for the family with the goslings—that must be the five geese swimming apart from the others. In July the three goslings had been fuzzy and yellow brown, peeping instead of honking. By August they had still peeped, but they looked almost exactly like their parents, except their cheek patches were darker and their heads and necks lighter. Now the goslings were young geese just like their mother and father, only smaller.

As the geese neared Andrea, one of the other adults swam too close to the family. A parent (Andrea couldn't tell the difference between the father and the mother) snaked out its neck and hissed, and the other goose shrank back.

Andrea realized why the geese were coming to her. "Food—food—food," they were thinking. The last time she had visited the bird sanctuary, she had brought a bag of bread crusts for the geese and ducks. Oh, dear, she thought. She didn't feel like sharing her lunch with them.

When the geese were within a few feet of Andrea they hesitated. She sensed they were confused. "Goose?" they wondered. "Bread?" They swam in little circles, weaving their necks through the air. "Not goose?" One even hissed at Andrea, showing its pointed pink tongue. The young geese tried to swim closer to her, but the parents shoved them back, giving warning honks.

They don't know what I am, thought Andrea. They've never seen a girl with wings before.

Finally the geese glided away along the edge of the pond, leaving crisscrossing ripples in the yellow reflection of the birch trees. They plunged their long necks into the water and came up gobbling billfuls of duckweed. She could tell it tasted delicious to them. Come to think of it, she was pretty hungry herself. It must be time for lunch.

As she walked away from the pond, Andrea felt her chest and back trembling like Jell-O. Flying was hard work. She put her sweater over her shoulders, in case anyone came along, and sat down under the spruce tree to eat her tuna sandwiches and apple and drink her lemon soda.

It was a late lunch—she could tell from the way the sunshine was slanting through the trees. She wanted to fly some more this afternoon, but maybe she needed a rest. She didn't want to overdo it. "Don't overdo it," Dad would say to Jim after her brother had been shooting baskets in their driveway all afternoon. "You don't want to get a muscle cramp."

So Andrea pedaled home, weary but happy. She would come back tomorrow.

As she pumped up the rise on Maple Street to her house she saw a yellow car pull into the driveway. Mother's car! Could she be home from Nantucket early? But then the car door opened and Jim's long legs in tennis shorts swung out. With disappointment Andrea remembered Mother had told Jim he could drive her car while she was away. Jim strolled to the kitchen door, swinging his racket.

By the time Andrea came into the kitchen Jim was sitting at the table with a half-full glass of lemonade. "Hi, sport." He wiped his mouth and then his forehead with the towel around his neck. "Man, it's sweltering. What are you wearing that big sweater for?"

Andrea frowned and looked around to see if Aunt Bets was nearby. "My wings," she whispered. "So nobody can see them."

"Oh, yeah, right." He took another swig of lemonade, tipping back in the chair. "Did you go to the bird sanctuary?"

"Yeah. That was a great idea. It was the perfect place to fly. I got all scratched up in the woods"—she pulled up her sweater sleeve to show him—"so I just went ahead and flew over the pond, but nobody saw me. It was wonderful." Andrea paused. She wanted to tell Jim exactly how wonderful flying was. But it was impossible to explain. He would have to see it. "Want to watch me fly tomorrow?"

Jim looked surprised. "Watch you fly? Well . . . I'd like to, but I'm supposed to cut about ten more lawns tomorrow. Got to earn some money." He drained his glass and stood up, chewing an ice cube. "Got to take a shower, right now."

Jim went out early with his friends that evening, so Andrea and Aunt Bets ate dinner alone together. "An *intime* little dinner, as the French say," said Aunt Bets. "Now, tell me what kinds of birds you saw today."

"Oh, lots." Andrea was glad she didn't have to lie. "A red-winged blackbird, two mourning doves, a whole flock of Canada geese . . ." She took a bite of scalloped potatoes and stole a glance at Aunt Bets. Three kinds of birds didn't seem like enough to fill up the whole day. "Let's see—some ducks—"

But Aunt Bets's eyes sparkled with interest. "That sounds like good fun. I think I'll have a try at bird-watching myself." She smiled at Andrea. "I want to live life in the country to the fullest while I'm here. It says in the paper the Rushfield Bird-watchers Society is conducting a nature walk tomorrow afternoon. How about you going on that with me, Andrea?"

"Well, no, thank you. I sort of like to watch the birds by myself."

Aunt Bets looked disappointed, but she said, "Fine. We'll compare notes tomorrow night." Her face brightened. "Compare *notes*—bird notes—get it?"

Andrea had to laugh. Aunt Bets was strange, but she was really pretty nice.

"Oh!" Aunt Bets slapped her cheek. "Speaking of notes, I should have written one to you after your friend called. Laura, is that her name? Lauren. She sounded like a sweet little girl. Anyway, she invited you to come over and visit tomorrow, and of course I said that was fine. She expects you about ten o'clock."

"All day?" Andrea was dismayed. She wanted to spend tomorrow flying.

"Yes, I believe so," Aunt Bets nodded brightly. "I talked to Lauren's mother, too, and she said you were invited for lunch. Isn't that fun to look forward to?"

Andrea opened her mouth to say something, then shut it again. Better not to argue with Aunt Bets. She could just leave Lauren's house early.

After dinner Andrea stood at the sink and rinsed the dinner plates while Aunt Bets put the knives and forks and spoons into the dishwasher. "Aunt Bets," she said politely, "Mother doesn't put the things with wooden handles in the dishwasher."

Aunt Bets slipped two more knives with wooden handles into the basket of the dishwasher. "Won't hurt them a bit, dear. I've been doing it for years. Just hand

71

me that sponge, would you? Now, tell me—I'm very interested to know what life plans you've formed so far. What are your dreams and ambitions?"

Andrea wasn't sure how to answer. "You mean what I want to be when I grow up?"

"Mm, perhaps." Aunt Bets skillfully swept crumbs into her hand with the sponge. "Don't wait until you grow up, though. You're never too young to get going on your dreams—and never too old. And never mind what other people think of you. Why, when Wallace— my husband—died, people seemed to expect me to fold my hands and wait to be carted off to the nursing home. What did I do? I dyed my hair and I studied and I got my realtor's license, and now here I am, quite a successful career woman." She snorted triumphantly. "People said to me, 'Mrs. Ducharme, at your age you have to be careful not to take on too much.' Do you know what I said? I said— 'Excelsior!' " She smiled warmly at Andrea. "I've always loved that poem. Do you know it, dear?"

"Just the part you said to us the other night." Andrea put Aunt Bets's lipstick-smudged coffee cup into the dishwasher. "Is there a lot more to it?"

"Oh, yes, several stanzas. 'Night was falling, falling fast—' No, how does that go? I'd have to look it up. Do your mama and papa have the collected works of Henry Wadsworth Longfellow?"

"I don't know," said Andrea, "but most of the books are in the living room." She led Aunt Bets to the bookshelves beside the fireplace.

72

"How silly I am!" Aunt Bets pounced upon a set of leather-bound books on the top shelf. "No, to tell you the truth, dear, I was playing a little trick on you. I gave your papa these books for Christmas twenty years ago. I wanted to see if he'd given them to a rummage sale." She chuckled. "He wouldn't dare. Let's see, now." Picking one of the books from the shelf, she flipped through the pages. "Here we are. 'The shades of night were falling fast. . . .'"

There were nine verses, but Andrea listened to every word. Not so much to what the words meant, but to the way they sounded, especially the "Excelsior!" at the end of each line. It felt like a bell clanging inside her. The poem seemed to be about the way she had felt this afternoon, flying higher and higher into the sky.

"'Still grasping in his hand of ice—'" Aunt Bets stopped, frowning at the page. "This isn't quite as I remembered it. He got frozen stiff as a board, for what? 'That banner with the strange device, Excelsior!'" She snapped the book shut. "I don't call *that* inspirational. What's the point in being a hero about nothing? You have to have a good reason, don't you think, darling?"

"I liked the poem, though," said Andrea.

"Yes." Aunt Bets replaced the book on the shelf with a firm shove. "We'll just remember the part that makes us feel like doing our best. Now then, did you have any homework to get out of the way tonight? So you can play with your friend tomorrow with a clear conscience."

☞ 6 ☜

The Rare Bird

Speeding toward the bird sanctuary on her bike, Andrea leaned into the long curves of Cross Street. What a relief to get away from Lauren. It was hard to believe that Andrea usually had a good time with her.

First they had started to make paper dolls, a family like the set of paper dolls on Andrea's bookcase. After a few minutes Andrea put down her scissors. "This is boring." Then they had tried checkers, and then card games. Andrea couldn't sit still.

So they took turns jumping on Lauren's pogo stick. They played on the gym set in Lauren's backyard, swinging and climbing and hanging upside down. Then they ate their lunch at the picnic table on the deck.

Lunch was the high point of the visit, but it didn't last long. Lauren stared at Andrea as she crammed the last bite of grilled cheese sandwich into her mouth. "How can you eat so fast? You used to be slow."

"Just hungry, I guess." Restless, Andrea jumped up on the deck railing and began to walk it like a tightrope walker.

The trouble was, there was nothing she wanted to do except fly. Once she opened her mouth to tell Lauren about the wings, but then she shut it again without saying anything. Lauren had laughed when Julie made fun of the birds' nests—what would she think of wings? What if she told Julie? Andrea didn't trust her.

Shortly after lunch Andrea couldn't stand it any longer. She dropped from the gym bars to the grass. "I have to go home now."

"No you don't." Lauren looked puzzled. "Your Aunt Bets said you could stay all day."

"Well, she changed her mind this morning." Andrea could see Lauren didn't believe her. " 'Bye." She hurried around the house to the driveway, where she had left her bike.

"You look stupid, wearing that stupid sweater all the time!" Lauren was yelling at her, but Andrea didn't care.

Now she was pedaling past the fence that circled the bird sanctuary. The gate was around the next curve. It was too bad about Lauren, but she couldn't stand another minute with her wings folded.

As she pulled her bicycle up at the gate a bobwhite's sharp two-note whistle seemed to call, "She's HERE. She's HERE." Andrea forgot about Lauren entirely. At last she could fly!

She dropped her cable-knit sweater under an oak tree and was about to leap into the air when she heard a racket like a chorus of bicycle horns above the woods to the north of the pond. Then she saw a long line of Canada geese, necks outstretched and wings flapping hard, skim the tops of the trees.

Andrea gasped and stood still. She had never seen so many geese at once. There must be fifty of them.

"Where?" they honked. "WHERE *where where?*"

The geese on the pond lifted their black heads and answered, "Here. HERE HERE *here*."

"Safe?" called the flock in the sky, circling back toward the pond. "SAFE SAFE?"

Andrea held her breath as she watched them. The noise of their wings whirring filled the air.

"Safe. *Safe*—safe," answered the geese in the water.

"Safe—HERE—here—*safe*." Still calling, the larger flock dipped downward. Andrea saw their black webbed feet push into the water, sending up fountains of spray all over the pond. Their wings beat briskly backwards. Then all the geese were gliding on the water. "Here—SAFE—*good* safe."

Andrea watched a goose dive into the water tail-up and then right itself, gulping strands of duckweed with a twitching motion of its head. She could almost taste the juicy, marshy plants in her own mouth. It seemed like a long time since the grilled cheese sandwich at Lauren's house. She stepped to the edge of the pond, kneeled, and bent toward the water.

Good grief! Andrea jerked back from the pond. What in the world was she thinking? Eat duckweed—

yuck! She'd better start flying. She had only the rest of the afternoon.

Andrea ran down the path, jumped into the air, and flew upwards with strong, steady strokes of her wings. She was a little cold without her sweater, but flying quickly warmed her up. As she circled the pond she flew first toward the sun, high in the west. She had to squint her eyes against the bright light. Then she sailed over the shining needles of the pines on the south bank, then across the cattail-choked ditches of the bog, then above the woods on the north bank. . . .

Andrea wished she didn't have to go back to school tomorrow. She wished the weekend could stretch out into a week—no, a month of swooping and dipping and soaring. But the minutes dropped away as fast as the yellow leaves dropped from the birch trees into the pond, leaving the branches bare and scrawny.

Later, when the sun was nearing the tops of the trees, Andrea hovered over the bog on a rising current of air. She knew she should be on her way home, but she didn't want to leave.

She thought dreamily about how many different feelings there were to air. When you were standing on the ground, air was air. But when you were flying in it, some air was thick and some was thin. Some lifted you up and some let you fall. She was the only kid in town who knew that. Andrea smiled, breathing in the pleasant dank smell coming up from the marsh. She dipped a wing slightly and flew in a slow curve over the woods.

Tiny voices, somewhere below. Andrea came out of

her dreamy thoughts with a start. She looked down.

A straggly line of men and women in jeans and windbreakers were threading through the pines south of the pond. Worse still—at the end of the line was a person with reddish blonde hair above the shoulders of her suit. Shiny boots flashed as she picked her way along the path. Aunt Bets and the bird-watchers! She had to get out of here before they noticed her.

Just as Andrea turned to fly back to the north end of the pond, Aunt Bets lifted her face. Oh, no! Andrea jerked her head away, but she didn't know what her aunt had seen. Her heart pounded as she flew full speed across the pond.

For a moment Andrea couldn't remember where she had left her oversize wing-covering sweater. Then she spotted it under a large oak by the gate. She grabbed it and was about to put it on when she saw something moving in the trees across the pond. Here they came! They burst out of the woods, heading for the path that crossed the bog and led around the pond right to where Andrea was standing.

Andrea panicked. Instead of putting her sweater on she clutched it in one hand and fluttered up to the highest crotch in the tree. She heard a shriek from the bog. Peering out of the leaves, she saw the tiny figure of Aunt Bets wave her arms wildly, totter, and stumble into the cattails. Then some of the bird-watchers hauled her out of the ditch, and then she was chattering at them like a squirrel, pointing over and over again in the direction of Andrea's tree.

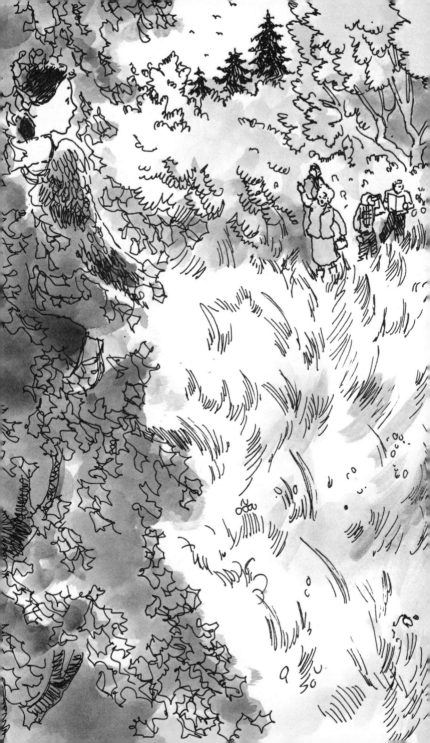

Oh, no. What a dummy she was! Aunt Bets had seen the wings. Andrea sat down on the branch, wrapping her legs tightly around it, and pulled on the sweater. Why hadn't she put it on in the first place? Then she would just have been standing on the path when the bird-watchers came along, and nobody would have thought anything was wrong. She hastily buttoned the sweater all the way up and pulled it low over her hips.

Looking out of her tree again, she saw the line of bird-watchers trot over the bridge that crossed the bog canal, along the path through the blueberry bushes until they were hidden by the trees on her side of the pond. Aunt Bets, staggering in her patent-leather boots, came last.

Then Andrea heard panting and the thump of footsteps on the path close by. The footsteps stopped under her tree. A woman's excited voice said, "I don't see any bright colors, but there's something white up there. Quite large."

More footsteps. "A snowy egret?" asked another woman's voice.

"Maybe a gull," said a man's voice.

Bending down through the leaves, Andrea saw three pink faces. Hands raised binoculars to the faces. And then they saw her.

"For pete's sake!" one of the faces said. "It's just—"

Then Andrea heard a wheezing noise, and Aunt Bets's voice gasped, "Do you see it? In this tree! A huge colored bird. It flew right to the top of this tree."

Someone snorted. There was a babble of discussion

as the rest of the bird-watchers came up to the tree. The first woman's voice rose above the others' in a snotty-polite tone. "There's something in this tree, but it isn't a bird, Mrs.—er—Bets."

An older man's voice said, more kindly, "Of course, you were looking right into the sun when you saw it, Mrs. Ducharme. Bright light plays funny tricks on the retina. Why, I once saw a great blue heron against the sun and I would have sworn that bird was orange."

Andrea was beginning to feel sorry for Aunt Bets. The bird-watchers all thought she was stupid, and actually she was right. And it was Andrea's fault. She eased herself down to the next branch, and then to the one below it, and so on until her feet reached the lowest branch, still high above the ground. She looked down at the people, about ten of them, gathered around the tree. "Hi. Hi, Aunt Bets."

"Andrea!" Aunt Bets stared up in amazement, one hand on the front of her tweed jacket. "How did you get up there?"

"Yes, how in Sam Hill did you get up there?" A white-haired man in a tan windbreaker looked worried. "She must be ten feet up," he said to the woman standing next to him. "Now, don't get nervous," he called to Andrea. "Just hang on. We'll get you down."

"Is that your little girl?" asked a young woman in a plaid flannel shirt, looking sternly at Aunt Bets. "You shouldn't let her climb up so high. She could break her neck."

"I climbed up here," said Andrea loudly, "because I

was chasing a big red and blue and yellow bird that flew up in this tree. But I'm afraid it's gone now." She looked at them reproachfully. "You made too much noise."

There was a dead silence. The bird-watchers looked at each other in astonishment. Aunt Bets said, "There! You see? I had sun in my eyes, did I?"

Everyone started to talk at once about herons and cardinals and parrots. Over the babble a young man with a beard called up to Andrea, "Maybe nobody else cares how you're going to get down, but don't worry, I'm going to get my ladder." He disappeared down the path to the gate.

"I can get down by myself," Andrea called back, but he didn't hear her.

The white-haired man frowned up at her. "Don't be silly, young lady. How could you get down by yourself? And now—be frank—how did you get up there in the first place?"

Andrea shrugged. "I just sort of scrambled up." She could see they were not going to go away and leave her so she could fly down. They weren't very happy with her, either, except for Aunt Bets.

"Hold on tight, dear." Her great-aunt smiled up at her. "That nice young man is bringing his ladder. It *was* a red and blue and yellow bird you saw, wasn't it? An extremely large one?" She looked around to make sure the other people were listening.

"Oh, yes," said Andrea. "I'm sure."

The woman in the flannel shirt glanced at Aunt Bets without smiling. "How fortunate that you spotted that rare bird," she said. "Other than that, this nature walk has been unusually unsuccessful."

There was a rustling in the bushes along the path, and the bearded man reappeared carrying an aluminum stepladder. "Okay! Lucky I live across the street from the sanctuary." He lifted the ladder and placed it so that the top step leaned against the trunk just below Andrea's feet.

As Andrea set foot on the ground, the white-haired man looked at his watch. "Well, I'd hoped to point out at least one or two more species, but I'm afraid the light is getting bad. I certainly want to thank all of you for coming on our nature walk, and we hope to see you next time. As you leave the sanctuary, you might note the waterfowl on the pond—the larger Canada geese with the black heads and white cheek patches, and the smaller mallard ducks . . ." He walked off, followed by some of the others.

"Thank *you,* Mr. Pockett!" called Aunt Bets gaily. She seized Andrea's hand. "Aren't you the explorer, shinnying up that tree like a steeplejack." Then her face grew stern. "But I thought you were playing with your friend. You didn't tell me you were coming here. Now, you really mustn't do that again, Andrea. Your mama expects me to keep track of you while she's gone. You must promise me you won't go off again without telling me first."

Andrea felt guilty. She hadn't thought about Aunt Bets at all when she left Lauren's. "I promise."

"That's right." Aunt Bets smiled, then looked down at her mud-covered boots. "Aren't I a mess? I must scurry home and change. My car's just across the street and down the lane. Oh, you have your bicycle. Well, come straight home, won't you, darling."

By the time Andrea wheeled up the driveway Aunt Bets was sitting on the kitchen doorstep in her stocking feet, wiping her boots with a paper towel. "Hi there! This is the final stage of my bird-watching career. Uck, did you ever see such disgusting slime? I'm too much of a city girl for this, I guess." Aunt Bets stood up slowly, her knees making a snapping noise. "Eek, listen to that. I'm also too old to go gallivanting around the countryside. But before I give up bird-watching forever there's one thing I'd just love to know." She followed Andrea into the kitchen. "What in the world kind of a bird was it that you and I saw this afternoon?"

"I don't know, but we could look in the bird book." Why had she said that? Of course the bird Aunt Bets had seen wouldn't be in the bird book.

But Andrea had said it, so she had to fetch *Birds of North America* from the bookshelf in the living room and sit down at the kitchen table with Aunt Bets to look through it. "That's it!" Aunt Bets pushed her reading glasses up on her nose and pointed excitedly at a picture of a bird with a blue head, yellow back, and red belly. "The exact colors."

"Oh—yeah." Andrea tried not to look surprised as she leaned over the page. Could there be a bird that looked like her? "No, just a minute, Aunt Bets—"

"Of course, darling, how silly of me. This painted

84

bunting is only four and a half inches long. The bird we saw was a big fellow—at least as big as a goose, wouldn't you say?"

"Yes. That's just what I was going to say." Andrea had a vision of herself gliding on the surface of the pond with her bright wings folded on her back.

Andrea blinked and shook her head. There was something odd about that idea—something like wanting to eat duckweed.

But quick, she had to think up a good explanation for the big bright-colored bird that Aunt Bets thought she had seen in the bird sanctuary.

"Hey, you know what? I bet it was some really unusual bird—a bird you wouldn't normally see around here. Like a parrot or something. There's some pictures in the encyclopedia." Almost babbling, Andrea ran back to the living room and returned with Volume P-Q. "See? I bet this was it—a kind of macaw. Somebody's pet that got away."

Aunt Bets peered, frowning, at the picture of a brilliant-feathered macaw. "Mm. It seemed to me it had longer legs than that. But the sun was in my eyes, as they so politely pointed out. Well. Now that our mystery's cleared up, I'm going to soak my old bones in a hot bath before dinner." She padded out of the kitchen in her stocking feet.

Andrea picked up *Birds of North America* from the kitchen table and started to read the introduction. It said that some bird-watchers had seen more than six hundred kinds of birds. It had taken them most of their lives to do it. What a project that would be—if she were going to find all those birds, she'd better start now.

Andrea began to go through the book page by page to see how many species of birds she had seen already. Canada goose, mallard duck, downy woodpecker . . . The trouble was that some species looked almost exactly like others. She would need a pair of binoculars to make sure of the markings on the wings and shapes of the bills and so on. That was why the bird-watchers this afternoon had been carrying binoculars. But not Aunt Bets, fortunately.

The screen door opened with a squeal of the spring, and Jim clumped into the room, leaving tracks of matted grass clippings behind him. "Hi." He opened the refrigerator and pulled out a carton of milk. "How're you doing, sport?"

"Fine." Andrea looked up from *Birds of North America.* "I'm going to start watching birds. If I do it all my life I might get to see more than six hundred species."

Jim poured milk down his throat, lowered his chin, and grinned at her. "Good. That sounds like a good way to spend your life."

"Don't be silly. I'm going to do other things, too. You know what happened this afternoon? I was flying in the bird sanctuary and Aunt Bets was there on a nature walk with some bird-watchers, and she saw me, I mean just for a second so she couldn't tell what I was." She told him how she had been treed by the Rushfield Bird-watchers Society.

Jim took a package of crackers from the cupboard and leaned against the counter, looking at her with his head to one side. "You really don't want anyone to find out you have those wings, do you?"

Of course she didn't. Andrea frowned at him. "I told you before, if they saw me flying, they'd get all upset. They'd think it was too dangerous for a kid my age to do." Andrea paused. Was that really it? Or was there another reason she didn't want any grown-ups to know she was flying? Something disturbing she didn't want to think about?

Jim seemed satisfied, though. "You're probably right. They don't trust kids to take care of themselves." He popped crackers into his mouth, munched, and swallowed. "One thing I don't get, though. You say they had to use a ladder for you to climb down from that tree. How did you get up in the first place?"

How did she get up there! Andrea was stunned, then outraged. After all she had told him. "I *flew. F-L-E-W.* You don't believe me, do you? I'll show you. I mean, I can't show you here, but just come to the bird sanctuary tomorrow, and I'll show you."

"Okay, okay, okay," Jim mumbled through the crackers. "Don't get so mad. I believe you."

"No, you don't. I'll *show* you. At the bird sanctuary, tomorrow afternoon." Andrea felt almost as upset as the day the kids made fun of her bird nests. She had trusted Jim, and he had just been kidding her along.

Jim swallowed and licked salt from his fingers. "Really, I'm sorry. I do believe you. But I can't watch

88

you fly tomorrow, because I'm playing tennis after school. Maybe the day after, okay?"

"Maybe," said Andrea coldly. She picked up the bird book and left the kitchen. She had thought Jim was really interested in her, and all the time he just thought she was a cute little kid. She'd never tell him anything again.

That night Andrea sat in the bathtub, lapped by warm water the way she had been lapped with warm air above the pond this afternoon. She was sitting at the end of the tub, letting her wings hang over the edge. She didn't want them to get wet.

Andrea's eyes were half-closed. Idly she paddled her feet in front of her. She thought of the geese paddling around the pond with short, powerful strokes.

Then her eyes popped wide open and she sat up, almost pulling her wings into the water. Her feet looked strange—something about her toes. With trembling hands she pulled her left foot onto her right knee and spread her toes. There was skin between them. It hadn't been there before, she knew it hadn't. Or had it? Maybe she was just imagining things.

Andrea let her foot slide back into the water. But she didn't paddle anymore. She quickly washed herself and got out of the tub.

7

Feathers

Monday mornings there was always an assignment on the board. Miss Silvano expected them to sit down right away and write a paragraph before regular classwork began. Today's assignment said, "I had a great weekend. First of all . . ."

Andrea took a sheet of yellow lined paper from the supplies shelf and sat down next to Lauren at her table. She wrote her name and the date at the top of the page. "First of all, I can fly!" she thought. She felt a surge of happiness.

Then she sat there, staring at the paper. She couldn't write down what had really happened. Miss Silvano would say, with a kindly smile, "Very imaginative, Andrea, but I asked you to write about what really happened." And Julie, sitting on the other side of Lauren, might grab her paper and start making fun of her.

What if she ran downstairs and outside and hid in the bushes near the school until the tardy bell rang, and then flew up to the windows of Miss Silvano's classroom and hovered beside the glass? She'd make a loud squawk and the kids would run to the window to see Andrea suspended in the air from her slowly beating rainbow-colored wings. The thought of the looks on their faces made her smile.

"You must be writing about something pleasant, Andrea." Miss Silvano was walking slowly among the tables, her arms folded. She leaned over and whispered in Andrea's ear, "Try to sit up straight, not so hunched over, dear." In a louder voice she said to the whole class, "Let's choose colorful words and phrases, boys and girls."

Andrea glanced over at Lauren's paper to see if she had any good ideas. *My family went to McDonald's for dinner,* Lauren was writing, leaning forward so her hair hung over her cheeks. *I bit into my juicy warm cheseburger and sipped*— Come *on,* Lauren. Fourth-graders don't get that excited about going to McDonald's. And *cheseburger* was spelled wrong. But Miss Silvano would probably like that paragraph. She seemed to want to read about ordinary things. Okay.

My mother and father are in Nantucket, so my Aunt Bets is staying with my brother and me, wrote Andrea. *She asks us questions. One question we couldn't answer was "What is a nine-letter word ending the sentence 'A banner with a strange device—'"*

Andrea's pencil stopped. "Excelsior," she whispered. Prickles ran up her backbone. She gazed past the

Swedish ivy and geraniums on the window ledge, over the lawn in front of the school to the trees across the road. She felt a longing so intense that she almost cried out.

Miss Silvano began to gather the paragraphs. "Before we start geography, class, did anyone bring feathers to school on Friday?"

"Feathers?" asked someone in surprise. Scott said, "Huh?" Andrea said nothing. Her stomach flipped over, and her wings twitched under her jersey and cable-knit sweater.

"Yes, the janitor found these lovely feathers on the floor this weekend, and I thought one of you must have brought them for a hobby report on Friday. You remember, we didn't have time for hobby reports." Miss Silvano held up three shining feathers: a large yellow one, a smaller blue one, and a fluffy little red one. "Julie, I thought maybe they were yours. They were found under that table. Don't you have a parrot at home?"

"Yes," said Julie, "but he's green." Andrea, who sat at the same table, busily picked at the wood on the tip of her pencil.

Miss Silvano looked puzzled. "I was sure they would be feathers from your parrot. Andrea, how about you?"

Andrea's breath caught in her throat.

"I wonder if they might have been part of your bird nest exhibit," said the teacher.

Andrea shook her head.

"Well, then, class, let's see what we can learn from these feathers, even though we don't know what kind of bird they come from. Scott, I want your full attention." Scott gave his neighbor one last poke and turned around.

"Now, one of these feathers is little and fluffy." She held up the red feather. "Feathers like these don't help the bird to fly. They help it—" Miss Silvano looked around expectantly. Twenty-five blank faces looked back at her. The twenty-sixth face, Andrea's, stared down at the Formica tabletop. She knew the answer, but she didn't dare say anything.

"—keep *warm*. Birds wear these feathers just the way we wear sweaters and coats. Do any of you have down jackets or vests?" A few children raised their hands. "Then you know how warm these little feathers can be." Miss Silvano put down the little feather and picked up the medium-sized and large ones. "This largest feather is a primary—it goes at the edge of the wing. And this blue one is a secondary—it goes over the primary." Miss Silvano held the feathers over her hand to demonstrate. Someone in the back of the room clucked like a hen, and Miss Silvano frowned. "Birds use these feathers to fly with."

Miss Silvano took a pushpin and fastened the three feathers on the bulletin board among construction-paper autumn leaves. "Maybe next month someone would like to do a report on bird migration. But for now, let's start thinking about our trips. I want to talk to you one at a time, starting with Lauren's table."

93

When it was Andrea's turn, Miss Silvano gave her a purple dittoed sheet to fill in. At the top it said, "My Trip to _____ ." There were other spaces like "I'll get to _____ in a _____ . It will go over (through) _____ . In my suitcase I'll take _____ , _____ , and _____ because _____ ."

"Are you still planning to fly to Florida, Andrea?" asked the teacher. "Fine. Here's a map of flight routes from American Airlines, and I also have a couple of travel brochures on Florida. You'll want to check books about Florida in the library, too."

Back at her seat, Andrea stared at the flight-routes map. This wasn't interesting at all. Just put your bathing suit in your suitcase, get on an airplane, and get off in Florida; that's all there was to it.

Gazing across the room, Andrea's eyes focused on something brightly colored. The feathers on the bulletin board. Who would want to fly in an airplane if they could really fly? A picture popped into her head of herself flapping through the air with a suitcase in her hand, and she smiled. Not exactly what Miss Silvano had in mind.

Andrea looked down at the paper in front of her and sighed. It certainly was hard to sit still and concentrate today. Maybe she should go to the library.

At the librarian's desk Andrea opened her mouth to ask for a book on Florida. But what actually came out was, "I want to find a book on birds going south for the winter, please."

Why had she said that? She was so surprised that her mouth hung open, but the librarian didn't seem to notice. "Birds going south—I think I have just the book for you, dear." She pulled a book from a shelf and handed it to Andrea. *Bird Migrations,* it said on the cover. The letters were printed over a photograph of a V-shaped flock of geese high above a marsh.

Andrea sat down at a table as if she were in a trance and let the book fall open. "Birds start to migrate when the days shorten in the fall," it said on that page. "They follow regular routes, called flyways." There was a map of North America with two lines of little geese flying from north to south. The caption said, "One flyway for Canada geese runs from the Great Lakes to Louisiana, 1,700 miles. Another runs down the East Coast."

Andrea felt too restless to read any more. Replacing the book on the shelf, she left the library. She was terribly hungry. As she ran back to her classroom she began to mutter a single word over and over. The word was *south.*

South, south, south.

After lunch and recess the low-math group went to the back of the classroom with Miss Silvano. Everyone else was supposed to be doing a work sheet of multiplication and division problems. Andrea looked down at her work sheet.

Instead of numbers, it was covered with meaningless purple marks. She looked around the room in alarm.

What was she doing in this place? It was closed in,

except for openings along one wall. If a dog attacked, she would be trapped. And the place was full of large animals, human beings. They were sitting quietly right now, but it made her very uneasy to be in this cramped space with them.

Nervously she tried to rustle her wings. She couldn't move them! They were pinned down by something on her back.

She stared, trembling, at the openings in one wall. She had a peculiar feeling they weren't really open—but they must be. She had to get out!

With a squawking cry she leaped to her feet, ran to the wall with the openings, and jumped up on the broad ledge among the plants and flowers. Her wings worked frantically to free themselves from the binding around her back.

"Why, Andrea. Come right down from there!"

The largest animal was charging toward her, its mouth open to bite. Andrea pressed against the opening, terrified—somehow an invisible wall pressed back. She could beat the animal off with her wings, if only her wings were free. . . .

The scene before Andrea swirled and refocused. Miss Silvano and all her classmates were crowding around her, looking up. Up? She was standing among the geraniums and Swedish ivy on the window ledge, her back against the window.

"Andrea, what in heaven's name possessed you to do that?" Miss Silvano was too surprised to be really angry. "Scott, don't you dare." Scott unwillingly took his knee off the window ledge.

At first Andrea couldn't speak, and then she saw Julie giggling and whispering something to Lauren. She had to pull herself together. "I'm sorry, I just—I got so excited because I saw a rare bird outside the window." Andrea climbed down from the window ledge, knocking leaves from the geraniums.

"Be quiet, class!" The teacher waved her hand at their laughing and talking. "What kind of bird, Andrea?"

"It was a—it was a beautiful bird, a big one with red and blue and yellow feathers. It flew right past the window, and I wanted to get a good look at it. I'm sorry."

"Hey," called Lauren, "I bet it was that bird." She pointed to the feathers on the bulletin board. "Don't you think so, Miss Silvano?"

"Mm . . . maybe so." Miss Silvano was looking at Andrea with a worried expression on her face.

She thinks there's something wrong with me, thought Andrea. I have to show her there's nothing wrong. She smiled at the teacher and shrugged. "Well—back to math." She walked to her desk and sat down. She was glad to see the purple marks on the work sheet were numbers again.

"Yes," said Miss Silvano uncertainly. "Back to math. Everyone in the Discovery workbook to me, please."

Andrea was suddenly shaking. She had almost jumped out a second-story window with her wings pinned down by her jersey and sweater. She had been thinking just like a bird. Was she sick? Maybe she should go to the nurse.

But all the nurse ever did was take your temperature

and, if you seemed to be sick, call your mother to take you home. Andrea didn't want her to call Aunt Bets. Besides, the nurse might feel her back and discover the wings.

It wasn't too long until time to go home. Andrea glanced at the clock. One more hour. Better just to wait.

When the dismissal bell rang Andrea was the first in line at the classroom door. Miss Silvano opened it, and the line filed out. Running was not allowed, but Andrea walked very speedily through the hall and down the stairs.

"Andy!" Andrea heard Lauren call as she pushed open the outside door, but she did not turn back. She just wanted to get home before anything else happened. It was a good thing she had taken her bike today.

8

Having Troublesome Symptoms?

At home Aunt Bets was sitting by the kitchen window, working the crossword puzzle in the newspaper. "Hel *lo,* darling. How was school today? Can you give me a five-letter word for *emergency*?"

Andrea didn't want to chat with Aunt Bets, but she had to answer. "School was fine." Her voice sounded harsh and strange. "I have a book report to do." She didn't, but it was a good excuse to get away.

Aunt Bets looked up at Andrea over her reading glasses. "Are you sure you're all right? You sound hoarse. And your cheeks look pale. If I were you I'd take it easy this afternoon." She launched herself from her chair. "Sit right down at the table. No, don't argue. I'm going to get you a nice little snack."

Andrea sat down. She *was* tired. And hungry. She

began munching the graham crackers and gulping the milk that Aunt Bets set in front of her.

"Oh, and here's a letter that came for you." Aunt Bets handed a blue envelope across the table to Andrea. "Maybe it's some good news from a friend."

Andrea didn't think so. Her name and address on the front of the envelope were typed—she didn't have any friends who typed. She pulled a sheet of blue stationery out of the envelope. At the top of the sheet AERO-JOY PRODUCTS, INC. was printed on a background of puffy clouds.

"Dear Miss Reve," the letter began.

> Worried?
> Having troublesome symptoms?
> Experienced aviatic consultant Hubert T. Vogel wants to help. Call toll-free number 1 (800) 339–2345.
> Looking forward to hearing from you,
>   Hubert T. Vogel, Owner and Manager

"Now, what did I tell you." Aunt Bets leaned toward Andrea, her face full of curiosity. "Good news from a friend, wasn't it?"

"It sure was." Andrea smiled at her great-aunt as she slipped the letter into her jeans pocket. "I guess I'll go work on my book report now."

She hurried out of the kitchen and up the stairs. She didn't feel tired anymore. Thank goodness Mr. Vogel's letter had come today. He seemed to know she was having trouble. He would tell her what to do about it, and then she could go on flying without being afraid of turning into—of something bad happening.

At the telephone stand on the second-floor landing Andrea picked up the receiver, took the letter from her pocket, and dialed 1 (800) 339–2345.

The phone rang once with a faraway sound. Then a man's voice answered. "Good afternoon, Aero-Joy Products, Hubert T. Vogel speaking." The voice sounded rather hollow—maybe it was a bad connection.

"Hello," said Andrea hesitantly. "This is Andrea Reve. I've got my Wonda-Wings on, and—" She stopped. Maybe Mr. Vogel wouldn't understand what was happening to her, after all. Maybe by "problems" he had just meant something little, like feathers falling out. Maybe these frightening things had never happened to anyone else except her. "You said in your letter to call if I had any problems."

"Yes, tell me. I'm so eager to help." His voice was low and soothing.

"Well, I've been flying and it's really wonderful, but—" Taking a deep breath, she blurted it out all at once. "I'm turning into a bird. I mean, I'm afraid I am." There. She had said it.

"You are!" For a shocked moment Andrea thought he sounded glad. But he went on quickly, "I take it you haven't told anyone else. You must be feeling very frightened and lonely. Is that right?"

"Yes." Andrea's knees were shaking. It was great to

102

finally talk to somebody who understood. And now she knew what she really needed to ask him. "I was wondering—I was wondering if I would have to take the wings off." As she spoke Andrea felt a wave of deep sadness, and then a wave of relief.

But Mr. Vogel laughed a hooting laugh. "Take them off! No, of course you don't. Actually I do keep the antidote, Ptero-terminate, just in case, but you don't need to worry. Believe me, I understand what you're going through. I understand completely. Your reactions are quite normal. You're approaching the stage of full acceptance, and that causes a great deal of anxiety. Once you get through the transition, everything will be fine. You're due for a booster dose of avesin— that's in the Aero-Joy Juice. Can you get to my factory in New Heights?"

Andrea had not really listened to the last part of what Mr. Vogel said. She was thinking, I *don't* have to take the wings off. I don't! Her heart soared and dipped. "Oh—excuse me?"

"New Heights, New Jersey. Can you get down here?"

"To New Jersey? By myself?" Andrea's heart sank again. "I don't think so. Can't you send me another bottle?"

"No, no, that won't do. You need supervision at this critical point." There was a pause, and then Mr. Vogel started to laugh crazily. "Vogel, you're a fool. A fool. She doesn't have to drive or take a bus or ride a bicycle. She can fly! Don't you see—she can fly! Oh, hoo, hoo, hoo!" The laughter died away suddenly. "Listen

103

carefully, Miss Reve. You must fly down to my factory in New Heights right away—tonight. I'll give you directions, and then you can fly over the expressway, following the signs. Do you have a pencil?"

"Yes." Andrea picked up the pencil lying by the note pad. "From the desk of Philip S. Reve," it said at the top of the sheet. Something Dad had said to her once popped into Andrea's head: "Never give a stranger information about yourself on the phone. It might turn out to be some unsavory character—I'm afraid there are people like that in the world." But this was different—Mr. Vogel was helping her. Dad would understand, if he were here.

"Now, where did you say you were coming from?" asked Mr. Vogel.

"I live in Rushfield, Massachusetts."

"All right. That shouldn't be too hard," said Mr. Vogel. "You're right by 128. Follow Route 128 to Interstate 95, and stay on 95 all the way through Rhode Island and Connecticut to New York. Did you get that? Good. Then take Interstate 287 over the Tappan Zee Bridge and into New Jersey. Just stay on 287—you'll see the signs for New Heights. After you get to New Heights, it'll be duck soup. There's a sign on top of the factory so you can spot it from the air. Dark roof, white sign." He paused. "And remember, you'll feel a hundred times better once you get your booster dose." Excitement crept into his voice. "I'll be waiting for you."

Andrea put down the receiver, slowly tore the directions from the note pad, and stood there for a moment staring into space. She saw herself flying with steady beats high above the expressway, slipping easily through the air over hills, over rivers. Mile after mile. Hundreds of miles. South. South! She wanted to take off right that moment.

Then she came down to earth with a bump. Fly all the way to New Jersey by herself? Don't be ridiculous. Mr. Vogel must be crazy.

But she had to get there! She had to! Andrea's throat tightened with anxiety. Something terrible was going to happen if she didn't.

Maybe she could get someone to drive her there.

Jim could drive. She would tell him what was happening to her. He would probably be annoyed, but when she explained everything, he would see that he had to help her. Mother had given Jim the keys to her car. They would have to leave without telling Aunt Bets—there was no possibility of explaining it to her.

Andrea wanted very badly to talk to Jim right now. They probably couldn't leave until tonight, but she just wanted to know for sure that he would take her. She ran back down the stairs, clutching the piece of paper with the directions on it.

Aunt Bets was still in the kitchen, humming and puttering around with pans and knives. There was a smell of onions frying. "Aunt Bets, where's Jim?"

"Oh, he won't be home until dinnertime. He's staying after school for one of his sports things." She stirred the onions with a flourish, as if she were cooking on a television show. "Need some help with your book report?"

Andrea realized that she was waving Mr. Vogel's directions dangerously near Aunt Bets, and shoved the paper into her back pocket. "Er—no, thank you. I wasn't going to ask him about that. I just thought of something I had to tell him." Andrea smiled sweetly, backing out of the kitchen. Rats. Double rats! She would have to wait until after dinner to talk to Jim.

Andrea walked slowly up the stairs, all the way to her bedroom. It wasn't anywhere near dinnertime. What could she do to make the time pass quickly? She studied the bookcase. A jigsaw puzzle. They always took a couple of days, at least. She pulled out the puzzle with the nesting wild ducks and dumped the pieces on the floor.

As she turned the pieces over Andrea thought about Mr. Vogel. She couldn't wait to see him. He had sounded so nice. So understanding. She pictured him with twinkly blue eyes like Mother's and white eyebrows and moustache. In fact, exactly like a photograph of her grandfather who had died before she was born.

Andrea found herself trying to jam two puzzle pieces together. She wasn't paying enough attention. But she had done this puzzle lots of times, and knew some of the pieces by sight. And she never jammed pieces. She hated to see people jam pieces together without paying attention to whether they were going to fit or not. Julie Dodd had done that once last year, and Andrea had told her she couldn't help with the puzzle anymore.

She decided to begin with the straight-edged blue pieces at the top. That was easy. As she sorted the pieces and fitted them together, Andrea felt herself calm down. It would be kind of fun to drive to New Jersey with Jim. He had been much nicer since Mother and Dad were gone.

It would be a big relief, though, to get this bird thing settled. Mother and Dad were coming home tomorrow night. Andrea couldn't wait to show them her wings. She imagined Mother and Dad walking in the kitchen door carrying their suitcases. She would stand there spreading her wings in all their glorious color, more beautiful than a peacock's tail, as they walked in the door. "Andy!" they would shout with delight. Their own daughter with wings! They would drop their suitcases and run to hug her, examining her wings and admiring them. Then she would take them outside and swoop up and down the driveway in the floodlights, showing them she really could fly. They would be so proud of her.

Oh, no. She had done it again. Andrea stared at the two blue puzzle pieces in her hands. The little knob she had been trying to push into the little hole was completely the wrong shape, and the cardboard had bent. The pieces dropped from her hands. She was ruining her puzzle. She'd better do something else.

Birds of North America was on the bookshelf where she had put it yesterday. Andrea picked it up, sat down cross-legged on the braided rug, and opened the book to the introduction. She wondered who was the youngest person ever to sight six hundred species of birds. If Andrea started now, how long would it take her? Her wings would probably help her a lot with this project.

Andrea read a sentence or two and stopped. She hadn't understood it. This was a book for grown-ups, of course, but she had been able to read it all right yesterday. It was as if the words were going in and out of focus—now she understood them, now she didn't, now she thought she did again.

Andrea put the book down. Impulsively she pulled off one sneaker. She looked at her sock. Just a regular white sock on a regular foot. Then she slowly pulled the sock off, too, and slowly spread her toes. She gasped. There was no question about it—the skin between her toes was up to the first knuckles. She yanked the sock back over her foot and sat there, breathing hoarsely. She had to talk to Jim. Right now. But he wasn't here.

Andrea pushed herself to her feet and began to move restlessly around the room. She wished she could spend the time before dinner flying. She'd circle her tower room, soar over trees and houses to the high school, and swoop down to buzz the tennis court where Jim was playing. Maybe then he'd believe she could fly. She liked the thought of Jim frozen in the middle of his serve, his jaw hanging open and his racket dropping onto the court. That would show him.

But she couldn't fly out in the open. There would be such an uproar that she'd never get to New Jersey before it was too late.

She could look at her wings, though. That would make her feel better, to look at her beautiful wings.

Andrea went to the door and locked it, just in case. Then she took off her hooded sweater and her jersey and turned her back to the mirror, looking over her shoulder. She opened and closed the wings, the way she had the first night. She was as gorgeous as a painted bunting, as brilliant as a macaw. The rainbow colors shimmered as she folded and unfolded the wings.

To see them better, Andrea picked up the hand mirror on the dresser and held it before her, turning this way and that. She folded the wings, unfolded them again— Hold it. There was something funny around her wings, between her shoulder blades and on her shoulders. Red and yellow and blue dots. She backed right up to the mirror. Maybe it was the color from the feathers, coming off on her skin. She hadn't been able to wash her back very well lately.

A voice came faintly up the stairs, through the door, through her thoughts. "Andrea!" It was Aunt Bets. "Dinnertime!"

"Coming!" she yelled back, but she did not move. Now she could see exactly what the dots were. They were tiny feathers poking through her skin. Pinfeathers. Feathers were starting to grow on her back.

Breathing out a shuddering breath, Andrea turned and put the hand mirror back on the dresser. Her face in the big mirror was still a girl's face, with messy ponytails and staring blue eyes. People said she looked like Mother. What would she look like tomorrow?

But she would be in New Jersey tonight, and Mr.

Vogel would take care of her problems. He had said he would help her. But she had to talk to Jim right after dinner. He must be home at last. Hastily Andrea put her jersey and sweater back on and hurried downstairs.

⌬ 9 ⌬

Fly There Yourself

During dinner Andrea tried to catch Jim's eye, but he seemed to be far away in his own thoughts. He ate two plates of spaghetti in absolute silence, while Aunt Bets kept up a lively conversation. The only time Jim showed any interest was when Aunt Bets said, "I see in the paper there's going to be a dance at the high school. Are you planning to take someone special, James?"

Jim frowned and stuffed salad into his mouth. "I don't know."

Andrea couldn't really keep her mind on what Aunt Bets was saying either. She was hungry, but every time she lifted her fork with the spaghetti dangling from it to her mouth, she saw a goose with duckweed dripping from its bill. She finally managed to eat a little by cutting it into short pieces.

After dinner it seemed to take much longer than usual to clear the table and help Aunt Bets clean up the kitchen. Aunt Bets was especially chatty tonight. "How are you coming on that book report, darling? Just let me know if you need some help. I was quite good in English when I was a girl, you know."

"That's all right." The last thing Andrea wanted was Aunt Bets's help with a nonexistent book report. "I'd better get to work on it, though." She gave the counter one last swipe with the sponge.

"By the way, what book are you doing your report on?"

Andrea was getting really annoyed with Aunt Bets. Now she had to make up a book title. But she could say whatever came into her head—Aunt Bets wouldn't know the difference. "It's called—*No Longer Human*." She froze in the middle of the kitchen. Why had she said *that* one? A chill clutched her stomach.

"Oh?" Aunt Bets didn't seem to notice anything wrong. She drew on rubber gloves and began to scrub the frying pan. "That's a story I don't know. Is it a very favorite of yours?"

"Yes. I mean, not exactly. It's pretty scary. I have to go do my homework now." Andrea hurried from the kitchen, concentrating on taking deep breaths so that she wouldn't start thinking about that horrible story. Think about talking to Jim. That was the important thing now.

As she reached the bottom of the stairs Andrea could hear Jim talking into the phone on the landing. He gave an uncomfortable little laugh. "Hi, Judy. . . .

How're you doing? . . . Oh, good. . . ." There was a pause, and Jim cleared his throat. "I was just wondering whether you'd like to go to the dance Saturday night. . . . Oh, yeah. Well, see you. . . . 'Bye."

There was a click as he replaced the receiver, and then Andrea heard him say three or four words Dad had told him not to use around the house. Jim was having one of his temper tantrums. He strode down the hall, opened the door of his bedroom, and slammed it so the doorknob rattled.

Andrea climbed the stairs and stood on the landing, thinking. Jim wasn't going to be in a good mood to do anything she asked him. Still, he ought to understand this was an emergency. It wasn't just a little favor he could refuse if he wanted, like when she asked him to help her get the money order. He *had* to help her now. She knocked on Jim's door.

There was no answer.

She knocked again.

"What?" he said gruffly. It sounded as though he wished she would drop dead.

Andrea opened the door cautiously. "Hi. Jim, I have to talk to you about something very important."

Jim was lying on top of his bed with his shoes off, holding a magazine in front of his face. "Bug off."

"No, really, Jim, something terrible is happening with my wings. I have to go to the Aero-Joy factory and get it fixed. You have to drive me to New Jersey tonight." She stared at him pleadingly.

Staring back at her unbelievingly, Jim let his maga-

114

zine fall onto his chest. "What? You want to go to New Jersey? You must be crazy. Why can't you wait till Dad gets home and ask him to fix your wings?"

Andrea came up to the bed and put her hands on the spread. "No, you don't understand. It's not that they're broken or anything. It's me. I'm—I'm turning into a bird." Andrea's heart thumped. It was such a horrible thing to say out loud. But she had told him.

Jim looked blank for an instant. Then he scowled and picked up the magazine again. "Hey, I don't feel like playing games tonight. Get lost, will you?"

He didn't believe her. "It's not a game! I *am* turning into a bird. Really Jim, I was thinking like a bird today at school and I almost jumped out the window. And there's *skin* between my toes—I'll show you!" She sat on the edge of his bed and started to untie her sneaker.

Jim placed one of his feet against her back and slowly shoved until she was off the bed, standing on the floor. "You're turning into a pain in the rear. *Bug off!*" He raised the magazine as if to throw it at her.

"Jim, you've got to help me!" Andrea tried desperately not to cry. He wouldn't help if she acted like a crybaby. Then she shrank back as Jim leaped off his bed and grabbed her by the arm.

"All right, I'll play your game. You can fly. You're turning into a bird. No problem. Just fly down to New Jersey yourself, without hassling anybody else about it. Especially me." He pushed her out into the hall, and she heard the lock click.

115

Andrea ran up the stairs to her room, gritting her teeth and wiping tears. She hated Jim. He wasn't very nice after all. She wished he would grow up fast and just get out of the family. She sat on the edge of her bed, stiff with anger, feeling the tears drip down her face. Her mind was blank.

But after a few minutes something seemed to come together and harden in her mind. She got up and blew her nose. She *would* fly to New Jersey. Nobody would help her—all right, she didn't need them. Her wings were strong. She knew she could fly much, much farther than she had flown so far. She had Mr. Vogel's directions. *He* thought she could do it. He believed in her, and he was going to help her.

But she couldn't fly out the window this minute. She had to plan. First of all, it wouldn't be smart to leave before Aunt Bets and Jim went to bed. Jim might not notice she was gone (what did he care about her, anyway), but Aunt Bets would be expecting a good-night kiss at nine o'clock. Also, she might check on Andrea before she went to bed herself, the way Mother or Dad sometimes did. That was a problem. In order to fool Aunt Bets, Andrea would have to actually get into her pajamas and go to bed. She would set her clock-radio for midnight, and get up again when Aunt Bets and Jim were asleep. But now she had better get ready.

Andrea lifted her backpack from a hook on the closet door. She would need food, which meant sneaking into the kitchen to get it. And a map. Mother kept road maps in the desk in the family room. What if there wasn't a map that showed how to get to New Jersey? There had to be. She had written down Mr. Vogel's directions, but just in case . . .

Andrea tiptoed down the stairs. At the second-floor landing she stopped and listened. Jim's radio was playing rock music. She crept down the second flight. The TV in the family room was murmuring. Aunt Bets must be watching something. Rats! Mother's desk was in there. Well, she'd just have to pretend she wasn't doing anything wrong.

Aunt Bets was sitting on the sofa with her feet up, wrapped in a satiny jade green bathrobe. Her satiny open-toed slippers were on the floor by the sofa. "Hi, darling. This is a marvelous documentary about mountain climbers. Look, that's Mount Everest—you know, the tallest mountain in the world. Care to join me? I'll move my tootsies."

Andrea smiled politely. "I have to do my homework." Then she paused. If she had to do her homework, why was she down here? "I need a map for my geography homework." That was a real inspiration. She pulled out the bottom drawer of Mother's desk.

Aunt Bets nodded pleasantly, her eyes on the screen. She was wearing green eye shadow and a green turban thing on her head, with curlers showing underneath it. Andrea was glad Mother never wore anything like that. Let's see, here was *Southeastern United States*—no, that only went as far north as Washington, D.C. *Cape Cod and Islands.* No. There must have been twenty maps in the drawer, and Andrea had to unfold each one to

118

make sure what was on it and then refold it the right way.

A commercial came on the TV screen, and Aunt Bets turned her head toward Andrea. "What are you looking for, darling? I'd be glad to help."

On the point of saying no, Andrea changed her mind. Aunt Bets wouldn't suspect that the map wasn't really for a geography lesson. Why should she? "Okay—I need a map that has Massachusetts and New Jersey on it." Andrea scooped all the maps from the drawer and carried them to the sofa.

"All rightie! Let's pull ourselves together, Elizabeth Ducharme." Aunt Bets hitched herself up on the sofa cushions, sending out a *poof* of cologne-filled air, and put on the reading glasses hanging from a chain around her neck. She shuffled through the maps. "*Eastern United States,* that should do it." She unfolded the map. "Yes, you see here, darling, this side goes from New York City (you'll have to come visit me sometime; I'll take you there) to Nova Scotia, Canada." Aunt Bets's forefinger with its dark red-polished nail slid up the map to Nova Scotia and down again through Maine to New Hampshire.

"Mount Monadnock. You wouldn't think it to look at me, but do you know I climbed it as a girl?"

"Really?" Andrea was polite, but her eyes were on Interstate 95, a red line wiggling south from Massachusetts to Interstate 287 in New York. She wanted to take the map and get on with her preparations.

"Oh, yes! I climbed it with my father, who never

mollycoddled any of us, and he wouldn't stop to rest. I was simply exhausted, but I was determined to make it to the top. When I was sure I couldn't take one more step, what do you think I said to myself?" She looked at Andrea expectantly.

"I don't know." Andrea shifted from one foot to the other.

"Excelsior! And that's what pushed me to the top of the mountain." Aunt Bets folded the map and handed it to Andrea. "Now you just think of that while you're working on your geography, and you'll do a top-notch job."

Andrea nodded and took the map. "Thank you." In the hall she stood quietly for a moment to make sure Aunt Bets was absorbed in the TV program again, and then she tiptoed into the kitchen.

Quietly she turned on the light, quietly she took the peanut butter and bread from the cupboard and made two sandwiches. The soft, thick peanut butter looked so good that she licked a big lump of it off the knife. It was delicious. She hadn't eaten much at dinner. Andrea sucked the peanut butter from around her teeth as she wrapped the sandwiches in plastic wrap.

What else? She took an apple from the fruit basket on the table, and a can of lemon soda and several Oreo cookies from the cupboard. She was so intent on what she was doing that she barely heard Aunt Bets's slippers *flop-flop*ing in the hall.

"Just thought I'd make myself a cup of tea during the commercial—Andrea, heavens to Murgatroyd! Surely you aren't going to eat all this food tonight? It's eight o'clock. I'm afraid you're going to have screamie-meemie nightmares, going to bed with such a full stomach." Aunt Bets looked sternly at Andrea from under her turban as she put the kettle on.

Andrea's heart had missed a beat, but then she realized Aunt Bets still didn't have any idea what she was doing. "Oh, no, I'm not going to eat this now. I'm just making my lunch for tomorrow in case I'm in a rush tomorrow morning." To prove it, Andrea took out a paper lunch bag and wrote her name on it.

"Oh. Well, that's a bird of a different feather. Good for you." Aunt Bets waited for the kettle to boil, then poured steaming water into a cup.

While Aunt Bets stirred cream and sugar into her tea, Andrea took her time putting the sandwiches, apple, soda, and cookies into the bag. It didn't seem like quite enough food, but she didn't dare get anything more until Aunt Bets left the kitchen. There, she was *flop-flop*ing back to the family room. Andrea yanked open the refrigerator and scanned the shelves hastily. Hamburger relish, milk, marmalade, lettuce—nothing good for trip provisions. Wait, there was something the shape of a dill pickle wrapped in aluminum foil. Andrea grabbed it and threw it into the lunch bag. She'd better get out of here.

In her room again, Andrea put the food and the map into her backpack. What else did she need? A flashlight. The one she had gotten for her birthday. She took it from her desk and added it to the provisions. What else?

"You always need tissues, no matter what," Mother

had told her the last time they packed for a trip. Andrea pulled several tissues from the box on her dresser and stuffed them into the outside pocket of the backpack.

She should take some money, too. She uncorked her pig bank, shook out a few quarters and nickels, put them in a coin purse, and tucked it into the pocket among the tissues.

Was that all?

Andrea went to the window and looked out. There was nothing to see in the darkness but the lamppost of the house across the street and the shadows of trees and bushes leaning away from the light. She pushed up the window, and chill air blew in. It would be cold flying tonight. She'd have to wear her winter jacket.

Except that she couldn't fly in a jacket. Andrea was not desperate enough to cut wing holes in her new jacket. Maybe Mother had put her old winter jacket on the top shelf of the closet. Andrea went to the closet and reached up to poke among the blankets and old games and Christmas books. Something slithered off a blanket, hitting her chest lightly on its way to the floor. She picked it up.

Oh, no. *Chilling Tales.* The huge shiny beetle, waving his feelers frantically. His thought bubbled up from his beetle head in a balloon: "It's me, your son!" His father and mother peered around the door, their faces twisted with fear and hate.

Andrea threw the comic into the farthest corner of her closet and took a deep breath. Jacket. Just think about the jacket. There was no jacket here. But she was staring at a low door in the back wall of the closet. That door opened into the attic. Maybe there was something she could use in there.

The single bare bulb in the attic showed rafters above and studs and insulation pads below. Balancing carefully on the studs, Andrea stepped over cartons and rolled-up pieces of carpet to a garment bag hanging from a rafter. She unzipped it, letting out mothball fumes. They made her choke a little as she pawed through the dresses and coats. Ah! A ski jacket. It must have been Jim's. It was much too small for him— Mother must be saving it for her. Andrea tried it on. The cuffs hung over her wrists, but not too far. It was just what she needed.

Still wearing the jacket, Andrea went back to her room. She took a piece of chalk and reached behind her first with one hand and then the other, making a mark on each shoulder blade. Then she took the jacket off and cut holes around each mark, narrow up-and-down oval holes. She took off her jersey and sweater and slipped the jacket on, easing the wings through the holes. She flapped them experimentally, looking in the mirror.

Yes, it fit just fine. But now the stuffing was coming out around the holes. Andrea took masking tape from her desk and taped around the edges of the holes. It looked messy, but so what?

At the bottom of a dresser drawer she found a jersey that Mother had told her not to wear to school anymore because of the stains on the front. She cut wing holes in the jersey, too.

124

Now Andrea was ready to fly to New Heights and get help from Mr. Vogel. She set her clock-radio for midnight, put Mr. Vogel's directions on the night table, shoved Jim's jacket and her knapsack under the bed, and put her pajamas on. It seemed strange, knowing she would get up again in a few hours.

Then she went downstairs to the family room to kiss Aunt Bets good-night and climbed the stairs again, wiping purple lipstick off her cheek. In her bed Andrea lay down on her stomach, as she always did now because of the wings.

She floated into a sort of sleep, more like a trance than real slumber. There was a room inside her mind. There was a door in the room. The door was open a little, and a sticklike shiny beetle leg was creeping slowly through it. Andrea slammed it shut and leaned against it, sweating with fear.

Then Mr. Vogel was in the room, smiling at her in a kindly way under his white moustache. He was speaking to her in his soothing voice. . . .

The radio announcer was talking in her ear. She was awake, and it was midnight.

Andrea shut off the radio, crawled out of bed, and pulled on her clothes. She eased her wings through the holes in the jacket and slipped her arms into the backpack straps, wearing the pack backwards so that it hung over her chest. She didn't bother to turn the light on because she knew where everything was. Besides, there was some moonlight coming in the east window now.

125

Andrea leaned against the windowsill. She didn't like the look of the moon, no longer full but not yet a half-moon. Like a mottled, lopsided egg. Her eyes went to the maple tree at the end of the driveway, but she couldn't see the owl there tonight.

Go. It was time to go. Andrea pushed up the window, pushed up the screen. She climbed out onto the shingles, scraping the backpack on the windowsill.

Then she looked back over her shoulder at her bedroom. If she'd never sent away for the Wonda-Wings, she'd be sleeping in her cozy bed right now.

Don't think about that. She forced herself to turn away, straightening her shoulders. She had to go to New Heights and get help.

Andrea jumped into the dark, flapping her wings. She flew down Maple Avenue to Winter Street. At the corner she veered away from the light of a streetlamp. There was a car coming—the people might see her. She'd better fly alongside the streets instead of right over them.

There was the school. The classroom windows were dark and blank, except for Halloween cutouts in a few of them. Andrea shivered and looked away. Of course she wasn't afraid of construction paper owls. She'd cut out some of them herself. But it was creepy to fly past them so late at night.

Winter Street led to Congress Street, a wider road with fewer trees. Andrea had to fly farther back from the street, ducking under power lines. Here was the plaza with the liquor store and the doughnut shop, and

there was the on-ramp to the expressway with its green sign:

$$— \text{128 SOUTH} →$$

Andrea hung in the air above the on-ramp. Route 128 to Interstate 95. Interstate 95 to New Jersey. In her bedroom it had seemed like a reasonable plan. It might be a long, hard journey, but she could make it.

She watched the headlights of cars on the expressway making tracks of light. It was a completely crazy plan. Nine-year-old Andrea, fly three hundred miles all by herself with a flashlight and a road map?

She dangled there in the dark above the streetlamp, beating her wings just enough to keep steady in the breeze from the north. She couldn't do it. She'd just have to go back home.

She couldn't go back home. She had to get help.

As she hung above the eerie purple green light cast by the arc lamp, some of Aunt Bets's favorite poem came back to her, slightly changed:

> "The roaring expressway is hard and wide!"
> And loud that clarion voice replied,

Honk.

≋ 10 ≋

South, South

It was a faint sound, but Andrea knew what it was—a goose. What was a goose doing up? She thought they slept at night.

Impulsively she flew toward the sound, away from the on-ramp. She heard another honk, louder than the first, and caught a gleam of moonlight on water. The pond in the bird sanctuary—this end of it wasn't far from the expressway.

As, Andrea flew over the woods and neared the pond, she saw the dark shapes of Canada geese moving on the silvery water, and she heard more honking. Through the honks came just one thought, which the geese seemed to be chanting in a chorus. South. South. South.

It reminded Andrea of a crowd shouting together at

a football game: Block—that—kick! Like the shouting crowd, it made shivers go down her neck. She landed high in a pine at the edge of the woods.

Andrea stood with one arm around the smooth trunk, pushing the feathery needles away from her face with the other hand. She had never seen the geese so excited. Instead of gliding across the water, they were skittering with wings half spread, leaving wakes of bright foam. The flock quieted for a moment. Then one goose fluttered its wings and rose up in the water again, and then they were all splashing and flapping across the pond. They must be getting ready to take off.

Andrea's own wings half fluttered, and her heart pumped fiercely. Time to take off. South. South!

All at once the whole flock of geese rose into the air and flew past Andrea's pine with a deafening beating of wings. The noise seemed to lift her off the branch and pull her up along with the flock.

The geese, with Andrea in their midst, flew up in a widening spiral until they were seized by a strong wind. Andrea was afraid at first, remembering how the wind had blown her away from the pond the other day. But the geese turned and sailed with it as easily as people stepping onto an escalator. The flock separated into a V-formation, and Andrea found herself flying in the middle of the left line.

In the excitement and loud flapping of the first few minutes none of the geese seemed to notice Andrea. But now that the flock was flying straight ahead in the

V, the geese in the opposite line began to look over at her. She could sense their uneasiness. "Goose?" one of them honked.

Andrea honked back, but not with quite the right sound. She felt a ripple of anxiousness travel up the flock. "Not goose?" they honked. "Friend? Not friend?"

"Friend," called Andrea. "Friend, friend." She tried as hard as she could to send thoughts to them of how much she liked geese—how she brought them bread and admired the way they swam. She was glad they couldn't see the bright colors of her wings in the dark. That would probably make them even more nervous.

The geese gave up trying to decide if she was some new kind of goose. "Friend," honked the bird at the point of the V. "Friend" echoed up and down the flock.

Then "South—south—south" took over again, a chant in time to the steady beating of wings. They were flying toward the moon, high in front of them. Glancing back, Andrea saw behind them a W-shaped constellation and the Big Dipper, touching the horizon.

With the north wind pushing from behind, Andrea didn't have to flap her wings too hard. And the geese in front of her seemed to pull her along, as if she were attached to them with strings. She knew they must be flying very fast, but after a while they seemed to be suspended in the sky like a V-shaped constellation, watching the earth wheel slowly beneath them.

She looked down through half-shut eyes at the little faraway lights of houses and streets and thought she could fly forever this way. The wind seemed to rush

131

through her mind, sweeping it clean of fear and lone-liness. It swept away thoughts of pinfeathers on her back and skin between her toes, of school and Lauren, of Mother and Dad and Jim and Aunt Bets. She forgot about Mr. Vogel and the Aero-Joy factory in New Heights.

She stretched her neck forward and beat her wings in time with the bird in front of her. To her right and ahead she saw the gleaming necks of the geese. There was nothing in the world but geese and the moon and stars and the air rushing past her ears.

Time passed, but for Andrea it didn't seem to pass. She didn't care whether it passed or not, or whether she arrived anywhere or not.

Then slowly she began to come out of her trance. It was more of an effort to beat her wings. And something was different. She was not in the middle of the line anymore. She was closer to the point of the V.

As she watched, the goose leading the flock fell back to the end of one line with a tired honk. The next goose on the right took its place. After a time the new leader fell back, and the next goose on the left took the lead. Finally there were three geese in front of Andrea. She was going to lead the flock.

Two geese in front. After a long time, one. Then the last goose in front of her dropped away.

For a few minutes the thrill of being the leader seemed to give her power. There was no problem about which way to go—the feeling of "South—south—

south" carried the flock onward like a current. But she had to flap with all her might just to keep up the same speed. Now she saw that the lead goose had to fly harder than the others. That's why they were taking turns.

Andrea forced her wings to beat up—down—up—down. But she was gasping for breath. Her chest and back began to feel numb, and in spite of herself the wings flapped more and more slowly. She was sinking. "South, south!" The geese were honking anxiously above her, beyond her. She was falling away from the flock.

Her strength was gone. It was like a bad dream, a dream in which her wings stopped moving. The aching muscles in her back and chest refused to pull anymore. "Help! Wait!" she cried, stretching her hands up as if the geese could catch her. The white tail feathers of the last goose gleamed faintly, and then the flock vanished. "Hurry, friend . . ." The thought drifted back to her like a bit of down.

The black ground rose up beneath her. She could barely keep her wings spread to ride the wind like a glider. Down here it was blowing this way and that, and she veered around crazily as it changed direction. Where was she, anyway? Was she coming to earth in Connecticut or South Carolina? What time was it? She had no idea, except that it wasn't morning yet.

Now she could see lights below, a string of moving lights like ants with headlights. Headlights—cars. She was drifting down toward a road. As she sank lower she could count the four lanes. Not just a road, an expressway. And most of the headlights belonged to trucks, not cars.

Andrea's wings ached. Her neck ached. Her body was like a sack of sand that she could just barely keep afloat. But she was almost down, drifting over the expressway now. Then she couldn't help it—her wings folded, and she dropped a few feet onto the hill above the road, just inside a chain link fence. "Ow!" She stumbled and fell on her hands and knees. Her legs, stiff from being stretched out for so long, weren't working very well either.

But stiff legs were the least of her problems. She was sitting in the weeds by an expressway somewhere hundreds of miles from home. She was only nine. She thought of her mother.

She thought of how, in a few hours, Aunt Bets and Jim would get up and have breakfast without her. Lauren and the other kids would go to school and sit down in Miss Silvano's classroom without her.

Maybe she'd never get home, let alone get to the Aero-Joy factory and get help from Mr. Vogel. Tears filled her eyes, blurring the sight of the huge green sign that hung over the road below.

The sign.

287
TAPPAN ZEE BRIDGE
NEXT EXIT

That was the way to New Heights! Wasn't it? Where were the directions?

Excitedly Andrea fumbled in her backpack. She

135

couldn't find the directions, but she took out the flashlight and the map. Yes, Interstate 287 was the way. All she had to do was follow the road signs, if she had the strength to fly another sixty miles.

But first food, she needed food for energy. Andrea pulled the Oreos out of her backpack and gobbled all six, one after the other. Then she had a drink of lemon soda, and then, still hungry, she took out the foil-wrapped something she had grabbed from the refrigerator. But after she had unwrapped the foil she could only stare. It was not a dill pickle. It was a chicken drumstick. A bird leg. She was afraid she was going to be sick.

Quickly she rewrapped it and stuck it under a big rock, out of sight. Another drink of soda helped settle her stomach, and then she ate the peanut butter sandwiches and the apple. Now she felt much better. It was time to go on.

Andrea couldn't fly nearly as fast as the geese now, and she had to fly much lower in order to see the signs on the expressway. The sky was getting lighter, but fog rose from the ground and drifted over the road, making the signs hard to read. Just as she reached the New Heights exit the pink disc of the rising sun shone through the mist.

She had made it. But now where was the factory? Dismayed, Andrea hovered over the Mobil gas station at the off-ramp. She had imagined New Heights as a little cluster of houses and stores with one big building, the Aero-Joy factory, in the middle. Instead she saw a sea of roofs, some large, some small, fading into the fog in every direction. If she flew too far she might fly right out of New Heights without knowing it.

She flapped slowly away from the expressway. There was a big building over there that might be a factory. No, it was a school.

To her left there was a lumberyard and a junk lot and buildings that looked more like factories. But no white letters. In the gray light all the roofs looked dark. There was a lit sign high on a pole, turning in the fog—

It was the Mobil gas station. She had circled back to the off-ramp.

Andrea was getting worried. Would she have to stop and ask someone where the Aero-Joy factory was? "Excuse me, I just flew down from Massachusetts . . ." No. She would look by herself a little longer.

What had Mr. Vogel said, exactly? "Dark roof, white sign. I'll be waiting for you." She turned and flew slowly over the roofs in a different direction, straining her eyes for white letters. She had to find the factory soon, before it was broad daylight and someone spotted her. Was that an *A,* half hidden by cedar trees? Andrea flew a little higher. A E R O—yes! White letters on a dark factory roof:

AERO-JOY PRODUCTS INC.
HUBERT T. VOGEL, OWNER & MANAGER

Andrea landed behind the cedars, inside the stockade fence surrounding the factory. This must be the back of the building, because there was no door here. Andrea hurried around to what must be the front. She would ring the bell and Mr. Vogel would open the door, his blue eyes crinkling with a smile under his bushy white brows.

⚞ 11 ⚟

Hubert T. Vogel

Andrea walked around the Aero-Joy factory twice. There was no door, unless it was a secret one like in a mystery story. She stood on the pebbly, weed-grown ground, wondering what to do next.

"Who are you?"

She looked up. A door had opened way above her head, and in the doorway stood a gray creature bigger than herself.

Frightened, Andrea flapped her wings and opened her mouth to hiss. Then she saw it was a man—not a very big man—in a gray suit, and she felt foolish. "I'm Andrea Reve," she said uncertainly.

"Miss Reve? You made it! Bravo! I knew you could do it." His eyes gleamed behind his round glasses. "I'm Hubert T. Vogel. But come up, come up. We shouldn't stand outside shouting like this."

Andrea flew up to the door, where there was just room for her to squeeze onto the sill beside Mr. Vogel. She could hardly believe he *was* Mr. Vogel. Where was the grandfatherly man with twinkly eyes? This man's eyes were staring and dark-circled. His face was round and flat, with a small, sharply hooked nose. He looked so odd she couldn't tell how old he was.

On the other side of the door, instead of a floor, there was dark empty space. It was the inside of a warehouse. Cartons were stacked on a platform below. Across the warehouse, at the same height as the door, light shone in a glassed-in office.

"Congratulations!" Mr. Vogel looked her over approvingly. "You've done so well—and you have so much to look forward to. But let's go to the office, where we can talk in comfort." A nimble leap and he was swooping through the dim air of the warehouse with his wide gray wings outstretched.

Wings! Andrea stood gaping after him. Well . . . why not? If he made wings, naturally he would want to fly himself. She just hadn't imagined him with wings. She jumped off the door sill and followed him.

In the office Mr. Vogel settled himself behind his desk on a round beam sticking out from the wall. "Please be seated." He motioned her to a chair.

Andrea sat down. She noticed his feet were bare, and his long toes gripped the beam. She quickly looked away from his feet. There was a filing cabinet on the far side of the desk. Behind Mr. Vogel's perch, shelves ran the length of the room. One shelf held nothing but bottles. Another held cardboard boxes of different

140

sizes with black stenciled labels: *Pinion-Pelts, Aero-Frame Support Systems.* On the bottom shelf, half hidden by the desk, something moved in a wire cage.

Andrea gazed around wonderingly. "Is this where you make the wings?"

"No, this room is just for storage and paperwork. All the testing, manufacturing, and assembly takes place in the room behind you—a combination factory and laboratory."

Andrea turned in her chair and saw a closed door in the plywood wall.

Mr. Vogel gave a little self-conscious laugh. "I call it my fabulatory." Then he looked intently at her, his eyes large with excitement. "But tell me how you came to fly. Tell me how it happened!"

So Andrea told him about flying in her sleep that first night, and about flying from the roof to the maple tree and back. Mr. Vogel nodded. "Quite a bit of courage, jumping off the roof like that!"

Andrea felt warm inside. She had been brave, and no one else had realized it. Mr. Vogel understood. When she had first caught sight of him outside he had reminded her of the owl in the maple tree, but now that idea seemed silly.

She went on to tell him about flying in the bird sanctuary, and how the bird-watchers had treed her on the second day, and how she had convinced Aunt Bets that they had both seen a tropical bird.

"Yes, yes, you did exactly right!" Mr. Vogel lifted his wings a little. His eyes glowed at Andrea. "How clever, how positively ingenious!"

Yes, Andrea thought, she had been clever. Mr. Vogel really appreciated her.

"Go on, please go on," he said. "What was it like flying south?" So she told him about joining the flock of Canada geese. And she told him about beating her wings through the night, gliding like a star with her friends. As she spoke her throat began to ache. She wanted more than anything else to be up in the sky with the geese again.

"Ah, fledgling," said Mr. Vogel softly, "flying is sublime, isn't it? And the best is yet to come." His lids dropped halfway over his round eyes. "Now tell me—when you called yesterday, you seemed very disturbed about some symptoms you were having. What were they, precisely?"

So Andrea told him about her urge to fly south, about how ravenously hungry she was all the time—

"Did you build up a fat pad on the wishbone?"

Andrea looked at him in dismay. "I—I don't know. I don't think I have a wishbone."

'Well, never mind. I thought you might have noticed. It would look like a sort of yellowish blob under the skin right here." He tapped the middle of his gray chest. "But of course it wouldn't be there now, because you would have used it up during your flight. Never mind. What else?"

Andrea stared at the shelves on the wall, trying to concentrate. She was so weary. After all, she had been up all night. "Well . . . I almost ate some duckweed from the pond. . . ." A little creature scurrying in the cage on the lowest shelf caught her eye. "Oh, you have white mice." She leaned toward them, charmed. "They're cute."

Mr. Vogel glanced over his shoulder. "Oh, those. I'd hardly call them cute." He hooted briefly. "Tasty is the word I'd use."

Andrea sat up straight. She was horrified. "You mean—you mean you eat those mice?"

"Do *you* eat hamburger?" asked Mr. Vogel, not at all disturbed. "What do you think that's made of? Do you eat fried chicken?"

Not anymore, thought Andrea. Never again. She felt faint with disgust.

"But we're getting off the track." Mr. Vogel's voice was low and soothing. "You were telling me about your symptoms."

Andrea sighed a deep, shuddering breath. "Yes. The worst thing is the skin between my toes. It's like—like—webs." She looked up at Mr. Vogel to see if he would recoil in horror, but he gazed at her calmly, sympathetically. She took off her sneaker and sock and stuck out her foot.

"Ah, yes." Mr. Vogel shifted to the end of his perch and leaned forward. "Yes, a definite web—up to the second knuckles. Very good."

Andrea could not believe what she had heard. She must have misunderstood him. "Good?" Her voice was faint.

"Certainly." Mr. Vogel nodded. "It's a clear indication that you don't have far to go."

"But it's awful!" Andrea trembled. "You've got to

144

stop it! That's why I flew down here, so you could help me keep from turning into a bird."

"My dear Miss Reve, calm yourself. You must realize that it's out of our hands now. Of course I know this is a very difficult period for you. I experienced considerable strain myself during the transition. But let me give you your booster dose of Aero-Joy Juice, and then you'll begin to improve almost immediately."

Mr. Vogel turned around on the perch and reached up to the shelf full of bottles. They were full of a rosy liquid, like the bottle in Andrea's Wonda-Wings kit. Except for the very last bottle in the row, near the filing cabinet. That bottle was filled with something black.

Mr. Vogel lifted one of the pink bottles from the shelf and turned back, shaking it up and down. "You're fortunate, you know, that you started young. The hormones are so much more effective during the growing period. Look at me, I've been taking the Aero-Joy Juice for two years, and I'm only a little more advanced than you after five days."

Andrea felt numb. She watched Mr. Vogel unscrew the cap of the Aero-Joy Juice bottle. "What do you mean—'advanced'?"

Mr. Vogel looked up, his yellow eyes unblinking. "Why, advanced toward the final aviatic state."

"You mean turning into a bird." Andrea felt as if she were falling through space.

He smiled at her in a kindly way. "Yes, I know, when you put it that way it does seem rather distressing,

145

doesn't it? But this is only a temporary, fleeting emotion. You are on the very brink of crossing the line between being a little girl dosed up with bird hormones and being the real thing." His eyes glowed, and he lowered his voice impressively. "You see, without the booster dose, you would become less and less capable of flight. You would never lose the wings, but you'd end up like a chicken fluttering around the barnyard." His voice was harsh and contemptuous. "Do you want that?

"But once you take the booster dose of avesin, it will carry you over the threshold as easily as you swooped from the outside door to this office. Instead of drawing from a supply stored in the crop—I mean the liver, your pituitary gland will begin to manufacture avesin itself. You will develop to your fullest potential. You'll have no trouble keeping up with the flock then!" He smiled at her as if he were sharing a wonderful secret.

Andrea felt a smile spreading across her own face. She was rising up, up above the fog with honks echoing around her, soaring far above the earth—south— south—

Then she saw her empty room at home with the books in the bookcase and the paper dolls on top of it and the puzzle pieces on the floor.

And then abruptly she was in a cage at the zoo, peering through the wire net at a crowd of human beings. She recognized Mother and Dad and Jim and Aunt Bets and Lauren, but they did not recognize her. She called to them, but only squawks came from her mouth.

"I'm not a goose!" Andrea screamed at Mr. Vogel. She was shaking all over. "I'm a girl with wings. And I want to take them off. You said there was something called Tear-o— Tear-o—"

Mr. Vogel's eyelids had dropped again, and he was looking at her thoughtfully. "To be sure, to be sure." He turned and stretched out his left wing so that its tip brushed the bottle of murky black liquid on the end of the shelf. "Ptero-terminate. However, it's misleading to say that you have a choice. Ptero-terminate is a powerful counterhormonal compound. It is toxic, though not necessarily fatal, and the side effects would certainly be extremely painful. I would not recommend it."

"But I can't—can't—caan, caaan!" Hoarse noises came from Andrea's throat, and she flapped her wings in distress.

"There, there, my fledgling." Mr. Vogel recapped the bottle of pink juice and set it down on his desk. "Let us take this step by step. I will tell you the story of my own struggle and triumph, and then everything will be much clearer to you."

Andrea felt frightened and alone and very tired. "I don't want to hear about you." She swallowed a sob. "I want to get the wings off."

But Mr. Vogel paid no attention. "To begin at the beginning, even as a boy I was fascinated with flight. While ordinary children played marbles and hide-and-seek together, I spent my time alone with kites, balloons, toy airplanes. But these playthings never satisfied me; I felt a painful yearning that grew and grew. I watched birds— Oh, how I watched them. I read

147

about them, studied pictures, dreamed about them."

"Did you collect birds' nests?" asked Andrea, interested in spite of herself.

"Nests?" Mr. Vogel looked surprised. "No. No, I didn't. Where was I? Well, then—I studied the attempts of men to fly. Not in a stupid, smelly, noisy machine, you know, but on their own. Icarus—feathers and wax—not at all well thought-out. Leonardo da Vinci had some clever ideas, but he too was missing the point."

"The point?" Either Mr. Vogel wasn't making sense or her head was getting very fuzzy inside.

"The point, the *point*." His voice was low and intense. "Real flight would never be possible with any sort of wings just fastened on the outside. They would have to grow on. They would have to become part of the body!" His eyes glowed behind his round glasses.

"Now I knew *what* to do, but not how to do it. The key, I felt sure, lay in modern science. I became a biochemist, and went to work for a commercial laboratory. It was there that I worked out the basic Aero-Joy Juice formula, the foundation of my glorious discovery." His voice trembled with pride.

"After that, it was just a matter of working out the details. There were a couple of false starts, but it wasn't long before I had my own wings—the same handsome pair you see before you." Mr. Vogel spread his wings so she could get a good look, and paused as if he was waiting for praise.

Calmer now, Andrea felt it would be best to humor

148

Mr. Vogel for a while. "You must have been pretty happy then."

"Indeed, indeed! But my innocent joy was short-lived." He scowled. "Making no attempt to hide my wings, I went to the manager of the laboratory. I stood before him as living proof of my earthshaking discovery and proposed to him that we begin mass production of the formula. And what was his answer?" Mr. Vogel glowered at Andrea. "What was his answer to my proposal, which would have brought him fame, fortune, and the gratitude of the peoples of the world? Hah! He picked up the phone and called the laboratory security guards. He wanted me taken to a mental hospital!"

As he talked Mr. Vogel grew more and more excited. He shifted a few feet one way on the beam, then a few feet back. "The fool! He didn't believe in my wings. By the time the security guards arrived, I had flown the coop—so to speak. Right out his office window, three stories up."

Andrea pictured the manager with his mouth open, peering out his window. "Where did you go then?"

"That very afternoon I left the state under an assumed name—Hubert T. Vogel. *Vogel*, of course, is German for 'bird.' I decided I would have to produce the formula myself, and bought this factory for that purpose. I also decided to share my discovery only with those who were ready to believe in it."

"Ready to believe in it?"

"Children," said Mr. Vogel impatiently. "Little chil-

149

dren. The unformed, unwarped, receptive minds. Children would believe me! So I advertised in comic books. And I was right. The orders started coming in—two, sixteen, forty-three, hundreds. The Wonda-Wing kits were waiting." He jerked his head toward the cartons in the warehouse. "Kits with brightly colored feathers, to appeal to the childish mind— Do you like the colors?"

"They're not childish." Andrea was indignant. "They're beautiful."

Mr. Vogel shrugged. "Of course my taste is a little more subtle." He spread his gray right wing and smoothed down a stray feather with his nose. Then he straightened up. "I put the address labels on the cartons and sent them out. Then, a few days later, I sent out a letter to each fledgling, offering the help I knew would be needed. I waited to hear from all the children who must now be soaring above the clouds."

Despair crept into his voice. "Oh, I heard from them, all right. And from their parents. They wanted the money refunded, they said. The kits were impossibly difficult to assemble, they said. They were going to sue me for enticing children to drink dangerous chemicals, they said. Do you know how many children actually put the wings on and flew?"

Andrea was sure it wasn't very many. "Ten?"

"One. One, out of all those hundreds of children, had the intelligence and perseverance to put the wings together and attach them. One child drank the Aero-Joy Juice. Idiots! TV-addicted ninnies! They do not deserve to fly!"

150

For a moment Mr. Vogel shook with anger. Then he calmed down and stared intently into Andrea's eyes. "Now you must see what I came to understand in my final moment of decision: I had no choice. Fate had chosen me as the bearer of this new development to the human race. Why else had I, out of all the biochemists in the world, developed the Aero-Joy Juice formula?" His yellow eyes, fixed on Andrea, shone fiercely. "You, too, my fledgling, are chosen. You will lead the other children to breathtaking new heights. You have no choice. And it is an enviable fate." He unscrewed the top from the Aero-Joy Juice bottle and held it out to her.

Andrea did not move. She saw Mother's blue eyes sparkling. She heard her say, "Human beings always have a choice." Andrea looked up at Mr. Vogel. She saw how short his arms were, how shiny and beaklike his nose was. He wasn't a human being. He might as well be . . . a beetle.

Hoonnk! Blank terror seized Andrea, and a harsh sound blared from her throat. She flung herself at the office door and sprang out into the dark warehouse, flapping her wings wildly. "Not friend! Danger! Not friend!"

For a moment she circled frantically in the gloom above the warehouse floor, and then her panic faded enough for her to remember how she had come in. But at that instant a gray shadow flitted past her and came to rest in the outside doorway. Mr. Vogel's widespread wings blocked all but a few rays of daylight.

Andrea wheeled past the looming figure of Mr. Vogel, back toward the office. Her mind was suddenly clear. There was no outside window in the office, no outside door. But there was a way out. She could see it from here, the black bottle of Ptero-terminate at the end of the shelf. She was still a human being. She still had a choice.

In a swift swoop Andrea reached the office door. She slammed it behind her and turned the lock. She ran to Mr. Vogel's perch, jumped up on it, and grabbed the black bottle from the shelf.

She glanced over her shoulder. Mr. Vogel was winging swiftly toward the office, disbelief and horror on his face. He saw what she was going to do. Hurry!

The bottle cap wouldn't twist. Andrea jumped off the perch and tapped the edge of the cap on the edge of the desk, the way Mother did with stubborn pickle jars. Oh, hurry. There, it was loose.

There was an odd clicking sound outside the door. Andrea looked up and shuddered. Mr. Vogel had lifted one foot to the lock and was picking it with a clawlike nail.

Hurry! The smell from the open bottle of Ptero-terminate made Andrea gag. Like liver and turpentine. She held her nose and put the bottle to her lips with a shaking hand. The oily liquid slid down her throat, burning as it went.

"Stop!" Mr. Vogel threw open the office door and lunged at her. "Idiot!" He dashed the bottle from her mouth, spattering the dregs over both of them. The bottle shattered against the filing cabinet.

Andrea and Mr. Vogel stood facing each other. She was gagging and touching her lower lip, which had been bruised by the edge of the bottle. He was shaking his head slowly and wiping black drops from his face. "Are you crazy?" His voice was anguished. Then a thought struck him. "Quick, quick, stick your finger down your throat!"

He wanted her to throw up the Ptero-terminate. Andrea stared at him stubbornly, her mouth tightly closed.

Mr. Vogel made as if to grab her, but then his arms dropped to his sides. "It's too late," he said hopelessly.

Then his face changed. Slowly all his feathers stood on end, making him seem twice as big. His eyes glared like the headlights of a car bearing down on her. "How dare you, you whimpering little *human* girl. You have received the most precious gift ever offered a member of our species—and you have flung it away like trash." His head trembled with rage. "Get out of my sight! Go, before I tear you to pieces!"

Andrea stumbled toward the door, stabbed by sharp pains in her chest and back. At the sill she hesitated and looked down. She hadn't given a single thought to falling since the night she first flew. But now tingles of fear ran up her legs as she stared at the warehouse floor. She glanced over her shoulder. Mr. Vogel was stalking toward her, his wings spread to pounce.

Andrea jumped. For an awful moment her wings wouldn't move. Then they unfolded and she flapped awkwardly, painfully up to the warehouse exit. Clinging to the doorframe, she heard the telephone ring in the office. She turned and saw Mr. Vogel snatch up the receiver.

"Humanity has spurned Hubert T. Vogel!" His cry boomed and echoed through the cavernous warehouse. "And Hubert T. Vogel spurns humanity!" He wrenched the telephone cord from the floor.

Andrea felt weak and queasy. A wave of pain seared her chest and back every time she took a breath. If she didn't go now, she wouldn't be able to make it over the fence. Jumping once more, she managed to glide just over the stockade fence and the cedars. Then she sprawled helplessly facedown in greasy dirt and chicory weeds.

~12~

You Got Found, Didn't You?

"Owww!" Andrea sobbed as sharp pains tore at her chest and back. The pain faded away, and for a moment she felt only the sickening churning of her stomach against her lumpy backpack. Then another wave of pain ran around her chest and back, as if she were being squeezed by red-hot barrel hoops. Whimpering, she rolled over onto her back.

She was more afraid than she had ever been in her life. "Mother! Help!" Her cry was weak, but she wasn't honking anymore. But it hurt, it hurt. Her breath came out in shallow gasps. She clutched at the weeds as she rolled from side to side in the dirt.

This spasm faded like the last one. Then another burning wave ran over her. And another, and another. How could it hurt so much? Was she dying?

Andrea braced herself for still another surge of pain,

156

but it didn't come. She lay very still on her back, looking up. The fog had lifted. It was a cool, overcast morning. A sweep of small clouds spread in dozens of rows across the sky, like feathers on a bird's wing.

Slowly, trembling, Andrea sat up. She must have crushed her wings, rolling around on them like that. Without thinking she tried to unfold them a little and shake out the feathers.

The wings did not move. They were numb. Andrea reached back and felt the feathers. They were still there, although they were full of grit and some of the quills were bent. But she couldn't move her wings.

Shakily, pushing herself with her hands, Andrea stood up. She could feel the wings now, a faint twinge on each shoulder blade, like a loose tooth. The Pteroterminate had worked.

Tears began to slide down Andrea's cheeks. She would never again feel her strong, beautiful wings lifting her into the air. Never again swoop across the marsh. When the geese flew overhead in their swift V, she would stand looking up at them with her feet weighted to the ground.

Andrea felt as though she had killed a friend. She couldn't bear it. She wanted to crawl under a bush and just stay there.

She couldn't do that. She had to get home.

Home? It seemed like such a long time ago that she had been a girl living with her father and mother and big brother. But home was the only place she could go now.

Andrea fumbled with the pocket on her backpack

and took out a tissue to blow her nose. She felt the coin purse among the tissues. If she could find a pay phone, she could call home.

As she wiped her nose Andrea looked up and down the street. Three or four blocks away, on the other side of the street, a white sign with blue and red letters turned on a pole. Mobil. The gas station near the expressway.

Andrea picked up one foot, put it down in front of her, and stopped. She had stepped on a pebble with her bare sole. Bare? She looked down blankly at her sockless, sneakerless foot. Oh. She had taken them off to show Mr. Vogel the webs. The webs seemed different—she peered more closely at her toes. The skin between them looked lifeless and shriveled.

Andrea lifted the other foot and took another step. Would Mother be glad that the webs were shrinking, or would she be annoyed that Andrea had lost a sneaker? "For pity's sake! I just bought you those sneakers at the beginning of school, Andy."

Andrea began to trudge unevenly toward the Mobil sign. She plodded past factories and junk lots, feeling like the clumsy barnyard chicken that Mr. Vogel had sneered at.

Here was the gas station, and there was a phone booth at the edge of the lot, behind a rack of tires. One foot in front of the other.

Just as she passed the tires a yellow car drove into the gas station and pulled up at the pumps. Andrea strained her weary mind to think how she knew that

158

car. Did she? At least it looked like the yellow Rabbit that Mother drove.

A tall boy in a windbreaker got out of the car, started to say something to the gas station attendant—and saw her. "Andy." Jim's voice was so soft that she could hardly hear him across the lot. "Andy!" Jim was running toward her.

Andrea took a few tottering steps toward her brother. He grabbed her and swung her off the ground, squeezing her as if he was afraid she might vanish.

"My God! Andy! You crazy kid! Are you all right?" He put her down, still holding her by the shoulders, and looked at her carefully. "Andy, did somebody beat you up? What's that blood on your lip? It's all swollen. And what happened to your shoe? What happened?"

Andrea just shook her head. She couldn't speak.

"Jeez, I was worried sick." Jim squeezed his bloodshot eyes shut for an instant. "I woke up in the middle of the night and I had this funny feeling, and so I looked in your bedroom and you weren't there. Then I saw the directions you left on your night table. I knew you must have sneaked out and hitched a ride down to New Jersey. Told a truck driver some wild story about how you lived in New Heights and got left behind accidentally, something like that, huh?" He shook his head, letting his breath out shakily.

Andrea looked up at him wonderingly. He really had been worried about her. But why was his face getting farther away, and why were her knees buckling?

159

As she started to slump Jim caught her under the arms and held her tightly, pressing her cheek against the zipper of his windbreaker. Then he shifted his hands and hitched her up, and she felt two jabs of pain in her shoulder blades. Something fell rustling to the ground behind her.

"Hey, your wings fell off." Jim laughed a little. "Well, that's something. You just about killed yourself hitchhiking three hundred miles in the middle of the night and you scared everyone to death, but at least you got your wings off."

Andrea looked back, holding onto Jim's arms. The wings lay on the asphalt, cupping slightly upward, their red and blue and yellow feathers only a little dingy. Her heart ached.

"Phew." Jim held her at arm's length. "You stink. Like—ugh—liver and turpentine."

"I do?" Andrea smiled faintly at the expression on Jim's face. "I guess that's the stuff I had to—to use to get the wings off."

Jim nodded. "What a miraculous solvent. I'm going to keep the windows open on the way home." He started to laugh, looking at Andrea. "You don't know how funny you look with my old ski jacket with holes in the back, and your backpack on backwards—"

She looked back at him. "You don't look so great yourself. You need a shave."

Jim just laughed harder. Then his voice cracked, and he stopped laughing abruptly. "You ding-a-ling. What did you tell Aunt Bets, anyway? For some reason she

161

just *knew* you must have gone to New Hampshire to climb Mount Monadnock." He looked amazed and disgusted. "She's looney. I tried to tell her I knew exactly where you'd gone, but she wouldn't listen. So I just left. She was calling the New Hampshire state police—she probably had them crashing around Mount Monadnock in the dark all night."

Jim was half carrying, half walking her to the car. He lifted her onto the front seat. "Just wait right here while I call Aunt Bets." He pulled a blanket out of the backseat and tucked it around her awkwardly.

Ah. It felt so comfortable on the soft car seat, so warm, wrapped in the blanket. She had been right to tell Jim about her flying, after all. He was the only one who could have found her.

As Jim headed for the phone booth at the edge of the lot, the gas station attendant strolled away from the pumps. He was a man about as old as Dad, with a weathered face and crew-cut hair. When he reached the place where Andrea and Jim had been standing, he looked down at something with a puzzled frown. Then he picked it up, and Andrea saw what it was. The wings. She felt a pang.

The man walked slowly back to the pumps, turning the wings this way and that. He came up to the car and bent down to the open window. "Hey, these yours?"

She nodded, choked with sadness.

"I'll throw 'em in the backseat for you, okay?" He opened the door and tossed them in back. Feathers brushed Andrea's hair, and she squeezed her eyelids down on tears.

The man closed the door and leaned against the window frame, peering at her with concern. "Some fat lip you got there. You got lost, huh?"

Andrea nodded again. She felt tears making wet lines on her cheeks.

"Hey! Hold the waterworks!" He made a funny-scared face and held up his grease-lined palms warningly. "You got found, didn't you?"

"Yeah." As she tried to smile Andrea could feel how swollen her lip had gotten.

The man lifted one finger. "Hold on just a second. I know what you need." He walked toward the side of the gas station, feeling in his pocket. Andrea saw him put change in the Coke machine, and then he came back to the car, opening a can.

"Here you go." He smiled at her, deepening the dark grease lines at the corners of his eyes.

Andrea drew one hand from the blanket and took the Coke, smiling back as best she could. "Thank you." Her voice came indistinctly around her lower lip.

The man went back to the office, and then Jim was leaning on the car window, scowling. "Man, am I in trouble. Aunt Bets called Mother and Dad in Nantucket. They'll be home by the time we get back."

"What do you mean, you're in trouble?" Andrea mumbled around her lip. "I'm the one who caused all the trouble. And I promised Aunt Bets I'd tell her if I went anywhere."

Jim shot her a strange glance, then looked down at his arm. In a soft voice he said, "I should have paid more attention. I should have helped you." He paused.

A grin crept over his face, and he shook his head at Andrea. "Three hundred miles in the middle of the night! You are some kid. You know that? You really are some crazy kid."

Andrea had never felt such warm feelings for him. She didn't want him to feel bad. "Jim, why should they blame you? You found me! They'll be proud of you. —Ow." It hurt her lip to talk too much.

"I don't know how proud they're going to be." Straightening up, Jim reached in his back pocket. "Well. I have to pay. Then we'll start for home."

As Jim stepped through the pumps toward the gas station office, Andrea gingerly put the Coke to her lips and took a sip. It was cool and sweet and fizzy. She had never tasted anything so good.

She sat there in Mother's car, breathing in its familiar smell of car seats and a hint of Mother's hand lotion. She looked out the window at the slowly turning Mobil sign. "A banner with a strange device," she thought, giggling weakly. She looked at the gas pumps and at the rack of whitewall tires and at the oil stains on the pavement. She looked at the two human beings in the gas station office—the man with the crew cut and her brother, Jim.

She was tired down to her bones, but everything she saw looked so solid and beautiful that she didn't want to close her eyes. It seemed she was already home.